# *AND*
# *LOVE*
# *ENDURES*

# AND
# LOVE
# ENDURES

a novel

by

## BRUCE K BECK

AUDACITY BOOKS
WE DARE TO TELL THE TRUTH
New York

**Also by Bruce K Beck:**

*Love and the Epidemic
(Audacity Books, 2018)*

*You're Sure to Fall in Love
(Audacity Books, 2017)*

*Produce: A Fruit and Vegetable Lovers'
Guide (Friendly Press, 1984)*

*The Official Fulton Fish Market Cook-
book (E P Dutton, 1989)*

This is a first edition from Audacity Books.
Visit us on the web at www.audacitybooks.com
For information about rights or purchases,
please email us at info@audacitybooks.com.

This book is dedicated to
the enduring memory of William Roy

## _Chapter One_

**If I had to put a finger on it**, or stick a pin in the time line, I'd say my eyes were first opened in Rhodes, of all places. *Rodos*. Not the Oracle at Delphi, but revelatory enough. This was in May of 1990. The Colossus was long gone, of course, but the island was inviting, indeed. A charming old town with narrow streets and wonderful cooking smells coming from every quarter in the afternoon. A climb up a low rise lined with little artisan shops, up to the Crusader castle on the promontory (a favorite of Mussolini's).

The entire trip was glorious. The ship docked at wonderful ports in Italy, Egypt, Israel, Turkey, and Greece: some places I always wanted to see, and others I had no idea I needed to see. And all we had to do was work a few performances—Bobby at the piano, of course, and I manning a follow-spot. When Bobby got the call inviting us to join the cruise, he accepted, but without much enthusiasm. I quickly cleared my schedule and started planning my wardrobe. I was stoked. He was indulgent.

Life had grown increasingly joyless in the previous year. I blamed vodka. Mostly. But it was maybe only the fuel and not the flame. Bobby grew more and more negative as I became more and more concerned. So when the call came with the offer of a dream holiday, I thought it was just the shot in the arm we needed. Bobby was indifferent, but he accepted. Bobby said he did it for me, that he wanted me to have the trip. I hated the context, but I loved the opportunity. And so I embraced it.

It was a Theatre League cruise. I don't know if they still do it or not, but in those days the League would book space on a Cunard ship and sell passage to its members and others who liked to hob-nob with stars. Those fares offset the cost to Cunard of the celebrity freebies. And of course the performers sailed—and performed—without pay for the sheer joy of travel. And the camaraderie, of course. A mini-musical, a one-woman play, a lecture/demonstration with songs, a reading of A. R. Gurney's *LOVE LETTERS*, all on our cruise.

The musical featured the West Side Romeo himself, Lanny Kirk. I had met him once or twice through the years. He was an old buddy of Bobby's. But I had never met his boyfriend, Rob. Not until we all converged on Sorrento. It was a lovely week before we sailed. It was filled with dinners in pretty cafés with a view of the bay, and an excursion to Capri (with the obligatory boat trip into the Blue Grotto at low tide). And a trip to Pompeii, as well. I had been there in my student days and was thrilled to be going back with Bobby this time. At the bread bakery—which looks so vividly functional—I helped the foremost tragedienne of the second half of the Twentieth Century plan a schedule for the workers. She was ready to put her back into it. I was merely enchanted.

There was also a harrowing bus trip along the Amalfi Coast, with merciful stops in picturesque towns clinging to the cliffs above the sea. That afternoon was crowned by a joyous luncheon in Vietri sul

Mare in a quaint guesthouse that clung to the rocks like a limpet. Lanny was particularly expansive and funny that afternoon. He was maybe the funniest man I've ever known. Which is odd, because on stage he was charming and had that glorious singing voice, of course, but the funniest man on earth? It rarely worked its way into his roles.

A quick example: We were boarding a plane for the trip home when I started to sputter about the lack of luggage space in the overhead bin, or something. Lanny said, "I think you should let go of that. It would make your face a whole lot easier to look at." I laughed heartily, and Lanny cracked up, too. And he was right.

Our final morning in Sorrento, we boarded a bus for the trip to the harbor in Naples. And on the way, we were treated to a private tour of San Carlo opera house (where *La Traviata* premiered). It's one of the finest opera houses in Europe, or anywhere else, for that matter. The perfect gilded jewel box, it also has grand proportions and excellent acoustics, apparently. It's all we got to see of Naples, but what a sight! And then we boarded the ship and settled in.

I decided on a seasickness patch, not wanting a repeat of my last sailing adventure. The ship's doctor dispensed them freely. What I didn't know is that they cause intense drowsiness, in some people anyway. Especially in combination with alcohol. At dinner I had such a hard time staying awake I was afraid my head would sink into the soup. I didn't manage to eat much dinner, but I slept like a log that night. The next morning, the patch fell off in the shower, and I was relieved. And the next two weeks the Mediterranean was smooth as glass wherever we sailed. I felt great the whole time. Physically.

Lanny and Rob had been together for about five years, I think. I'm not sure how they met. I think Rob was living in California at the time. He was medium-sized, nicely built, and handsome like a 1970's porn star. He's just a few years younger than I am. And there's that smile that gives him those endearing dimples. Rob's smile is so radiant, it could melt a glacier. I wasn't certain about him when we first met. Hot, yes. But was the sweetness real? I wondered. Yes, actually. What you see is what you get. Rob is one of those rare people who is entirely present in the moment. And if you're with him, then he's yours. For that period of time. But you'd better cherish it, because there might not be another. Plans? Forget it. The past and the future don't exist. There is only now.

In our first few days on the ship, I went to Lanny and Rob's stateroom one afternoon while we were at sea. Bobby had asked me to get something or other. The performers were rehearsing. And there Rob and I were, just the two of us. In a stateroom. With beds. In the middle of the Mediterranean. I fetched the papers, or whatever my errand was, and Rob and I laughed about something or other, probably one of the other passengers. And then we were in each other's arms. And then Rob kissed me. I was shocked. But I kissed him back, of course. We laughed and kissed some more. And then some more. Where, indeed, was it leading? Was this hunky guy really coming on to me? Or was he naturally affectionate? Were we going to tear off our clothes and have at it? Or did Rob just enjoy easy contact with his friends?

I can't say exactly what I was thinking, but perhaps I couldn't imagine this hottie taking an interest in li'l ol' me. Or maybe I didn't want to overstay my welcome. Or misinterpret his advances. But whatever was going on in my head, I thanked Rob for the papers and headed back to our cabin, trying to arrange my erection so it wouldn't show in my jeans. Fat chance. Luckily, the papers were large enough to hold casually in front of me.

My head buzzed for a while, of course. How far, I wondered, had Rob intended to go? If indeed he had any intentions at all. Was I rude? No one likes an incomplete pass. Had I been sensible and loyal, or had I just missed out on a lovely moment? Opportunity like that knocks only once, I think. If I really wanted answers to my questions, I'd have to ask Rob, I suppose. And I haven't seen him in years. Maybe it's better to just leave it filed away in that quiet place where the sweet memories live. It's a much nicer file to reopen than the ugly memories, of which there are just as many.

Speaking of where the sweet memories live, our first Eastern port was Alexandria. We traveled overland to Cairo, and Giza, and all of that, of course. Papyrus shop? Check. Cairo Museum? Check. Rob managed to attract the attention of two museum guards. At Rob's urging I walked back through a section I had already viewed only to pass a guard who winked and growled. Surely these hot guys were not turning tricks in the men's room in the Cairo Museum, on the same floor as King Tut, in the heartland of homophobia. Or were they? Entrapment? Who the fuck knows? But whatever they were doing, they provided considerable entertainment for these tourists. And so did Tut, of course.

Camel ride up to the Great Pyramid? Check. They dressed us in robes and headgear for the trip, of course. I said to Lanny, "You look good, but it's more Bernice than burnoose." I've always been proud of that one. Sound-and-light show in the Valley of the Kings? Check. Alexander Scourby's booming voice (from the grave, yet) rattling what's left of the Sphinx. And then dinner at Mena House with veiled belly dancers. Check.

Our final day in Alexandria was my favorite. Bobby wanted to stay in and get some work done, so Lanny, Rob, and I headed out to see the city. Right away they found a guy with a little horse-drawn cart who was available for a city tour. The driver was charming, actually, and so was his horse. And we stopped to take pictures of all five of us now and then. He took us through the old quarter, I guess. We made stops at his sister-in-law's souvenir shop, etc. But we also got to see some small museum/shrines and a fair bit of the real city of Alexandria. I was enchanted. And spending the day with Lanny and Rob was delightful.

We sailed from Alexandria just before sunset. And I'm so glad Bobby and I decided to go on deck to watch the departure. What a harbor! What a port. So vast it makes New York Harbor look like a backwater. Except for Lady Liberty, of course. She's pretty nifty. And even Alexandria doesn't have her.

There were other flirtations that trip, of a less wholesome nature. Quickies in the shower after exercise class. A three-way in a bed that was only big enough for one. There was a passenger named Harvey who had a crush on me. He was traveling with his mother and not his boyfriend that trip, so he felt free to court me. Harvey's mother was great fun—animated, outgoing. Harvey told me his father used to say, "If I had murdered her the first time I wanted to, I'd be out by now!" Harvey was insistent, but I played by the rules. More or less.

I never had a romantic encounter with Lanny, but there was an odd conversation at the end of the cruise, after we had all disembarked at the ancient port of Piraeus and settled into a comfortable bargain hotel in a little resort north of Athens. I hope you'll permit me a digression, because that hotel afforded me one of my most precious memories:

One morning I stepped into the tub and threw open the window. It was late May, the sun was shining, a slight breeze rustled the trees that were trying to obscure my view of the Aegean, and a house just to the right was covered with bougainvillea and other flowering bushes in exotic colors. I stood in the shower with hot water pouring down my back and drank in the view and the scents of spring and flowers and an ancient sea. And I had a moment of complete happiness. They are, after all, relatively rare.

But, back to my narrative. We all met one morning for a tour of the Acropolis. Of course. What else on a first visit to Athens? That was the tour where we had a wonderful guide, and Bobby said, "Ask her about your shirt."

Just as we were about to step through the gate that reveals that stunning first view of the Parthenon, I asked our guide, "What does this say?" pointing to the writing on the shirt I had bought in Crete a few days before.

"It says you are waiting for your husband to return from the Trojan Wars," she said. And sure enough, there was Penelope at her spinning. I decided I could wear that shirt, even in Greece. It seemed loyal and good. And I still own it. And I still chuckle whenever I come across it in my closet.

But a few minutes earlier, as we headed up the hill, Lanny and I happened to be walking together when he said, "Rob and I were talking about you two, and we were trying to decide who's the top. I said you are."

I was more surprised to learn that Lanny and Rob had been talking about us at all than that they had been speculating about our sexual roles. I didn't have a ready answer. Even for myself. So I said, "I don't think about us that way," or something equally lame. Lanny told me that he used to like to body-worship muscle guys, before he and Rob got together. And then we were nearing the top of the hill, and that was pretty much the end of the conversation. It didn't occur to me until much later that I had missed a chance to share something intimate with a deeply delightful, richly complex, and exquisitely talented man.

I knew Lanny was Positive. I knew he had had a few illnesses. He looked a bit gray, but otherwise nearly 100%. I'm guessing that he had reached a point in his life where he wanted to cut through the bullshit and get right to it. Not that he hadn't always been up-front. But he offered his true self to me while the two of us were walking together on that ancient path. Up to the fucking Parthenon, for Christ's sake. And I was unable to respond. I was too self-conscious to just laugh, and love him, and invite him into my heart. Which would have been enough. Clever was not required. I guess I had already cleared some screening hurdles, in our weeks together, or he wouldn't have bothered to speak to me at all. But when he served, I fumbled. Game over. And I will always feel diminished by that failure.

But Rhodes. Yes, Rhodes. This part is really hard to write. But I don't think my story makes much sense without it. We docked at Rhodes in the middle of our second week, and planned an excursion with two guys on the cruise we had become chummy with. They were a DC doctor and his boyfriend who worked at the State Department. They were fun. We were all looking forward to going ashore.

We took in the sights in the harbor area, and we climbed up the hill and took some pictures, clowning with the statuary. Tourist stuff. The guys wanted to rent motorbikes to explore the island. I had never been able to get Bobby on any sort of bike in our fifteen years together. But to my surprise, he said, "Sure." Contracts were signed, followed by some quick operating instructions, and then we were on our way. I was driving, of course, and Bobby hopped on behind and put his arms around my middle. Maybe the guys doubled up on one bike, too, or maybe they rode separately. It doesn't matter. They took the lead, after promising not to go too fast. And we were off.

It really is quite a beautiful island. I would have enjoyed seeing it more if I hadn't had the responsibility of driving. I'm not saying that the memory of a crack-up in my high school days haunted me, only that I didn't really like bikes all that much more than Bobby did. And there we were. The guys were driving a bit faster than I would have liked, but I kept up with them. We stopped once or twice to take in the view and then roared off to new vistas.

Bobby seemed restless. That was my first impression. But then as we were speeding along a sort of cliffside road above the beach on the north coast, he became actually fidgety. I asked him to be still. He became even more animated. It took all my concentration to keep us on the road. And at that moment, I realized, somewhere in my consciousness, that Bobby would have been happy to tumble off that cliff to his death. And take me with him.

There, I've said it. It seems so unthinkable—then as now—but that was the reality of our lives in those years. Mostly I stuffed it. We finished our tour of Rhodes on another ugly note, however: There was a big piece of wood in the middle of the road that I slowed down for and tried to avoid. But I still hit it, at slow speed, and we spun out just enough for me to get a nasty scrape on one leg. Bobby was uninjured. We walked the bike—also uninjured, fortunately—back to the rental place. The great, solid mass of the ship looked very inviting as we headed back to get ready for dinner.

So, underneath the brightness and warmth of our festive springtime adventure there was a darkness that seemed cold and inescapable. When it caught my attention, that is. Much of the time I felt as light and joyous as we all deserved to feel. But the darkness had begun to creep in the year before, at least. It was mostly about vodka. Lord knows, I was doing my best to keep up with Bobby. No mean feat.

But I had relative youth on my side. And Bobby, twenty years my senior, had outgrown the luxury of being able to punish his body with impunity. Vodka began to show—in his face, in his mood, in his soul. It hadn't begun to show in his work. Yet. I think. That would come later. I may not be the best judge of these things, considering my proximity to the problem. And my participation in it. But I'll give the telling of it my best shot.

After we returned from the Mediterranean trip, it was as if Bobby dropped all pretense of happiness. He had promised me the holiday, and now that it was done, he could let go. He said as much. It was horrible to watch his sense of defeat. And he wanted it to be my fault. He had his reasons, of course. Nothing happens in a vacuum.

## Chapter Two

**I know I told you** it was mostly about vodka. And that's the truth. But there was a precipitating event. There always is, I guess. And as much as I hate having to recall it, how can I explain the present without the past?

One afternoon in the late '80s, Bobby got a call from an old buddy, who was one third of the most famous singing sister act of the 1930s and '40s. She asked if she could give Bobby's phone number to Jim Alexander. He needed a composer for a show he was writing. Bobby agreed, Jim called, and Bobby went around the corner to meet with him. Jim had two-and-a-half floors of a medium-sized apartment building on Sutton Place. Very impressive. Jim's two or three hit songs in the fifties earned him enough money so that he could invest in LA real estate—which returned a fortune.

Bobby said, "Jim is rich, and he knows everybody. Maybe I should just do it, for the money. Isn't that what other people do?" There were red flags, of course. Jim hadn't written anything of interest in the last thirty years, as far as we knew. The biggest and brightest red flag? Two other composers had already worked with Jim on this project and then backed out. Bobby said yes. The work began.

Bobby went to Jim's a few afternoons a week. Jim shared his home with his boyfriend (and adoptive son—that was the safest way to sew up inheritance in the years before Marriage.) The "son" was a decorator—and a very good one. The apartment was quite beautiful. I was there a few times. Every room I saw was richly comfortable and inviting. The living room, which was only used for the most formal occasions, featured a grand piano in the front window flanked by two marble kouroi. Hellenistic, I think, is the correct term for the naturalistic modeling and voluptuous curves that define these boys. Jim owned not one but *two* ancient celebrations of young male beauty. They were a bit battered but still breathtaking more than two thousand years after they were sculpted.

Songs were crafted. Bobby was not happy with how things were going. "There's only so much I can do with Jim's lyrics. I wish I could just improve them, but I'm stuck with what he gives me. And believe me, it's not great." And then, in a few months, Jim felt he had enough material to demonstrate to a respected actress he wanted to consider the title role, and to a respected director he wanted to consider directing the thing. Jim could get anyone's attention. A trip was planned, demonstrations scheduled, reservations made, tickets bought.

"Bobby," I said, "how can you go to LA and demonstrate those songs when you don't believe in them? Never mind [the actress]. You don't know her, and she's nothing to your career, really. But [the director]? You know him. You respect him. He's a big fan of yours right now, and I think you should keep it that way."

"How can I get out of it? What would I tell Jim?"

"That's the easy part," I said. "Once you've decided not to go, we'll find some plausible explanation for Jim, and then it's done. End of story. He's a big boy. He'll deal with it."

"But I told him I'll go."

"But if you don't believe in the show, and you think you'll be humiliated by the experience, then don't go!" I pleaded with him to let me help him avoid the pain. This went on for days with no solution in sight. And in the end, Bobby went to California, demonstrated the new show for the respected actress and the respected director, and felt deeply humiliated. But what was worse than the professional pain he felt was his conviction that—for the first time in our fourteen years together—he did not have my support.

Was that the reality of the situation? It was for him. I thought my actions were all about love and support. That was how it felt at the time. Still does, more or less. Not that I couldn't have handled it better. But Bobby's world was quite different. Even at the risk of sounding melodramatic, I have to tell you that Bobby returned from that trip a broken man. And Mr. Fix-it here couldn't fix shit.

Bobby's morale didn't improve after the California trip. In fact it got worse. And his tremor increased, so that he needed more vodka to tame it. And the more vodka, the stronger the tremor. Until he was drinking most of the day. I even took him to a neurologist once, asking the doctor to treat Bobby's tremor so that he could return to more recreational vodka use.

The doctor examined him and asked the usual questions. And then he said, "Your tremor is caused by alcohol, and there are no drugs to treat it. The only way to reduce it is to reduce your vodka intake. Mr. James, you're a lucky man to have a friend looking out for you. I think you should listen to him." I had my doubts about how much of that information Bobby actually absorbed. He was skilled at selective hearing, like the rest of us. And the fact that the doctor praised my concern seemed likely to backfire.

I would call the next year a steady decline. It wasn't all unrelievedly grim, however. We had some fun times, like when two friends ordered up a rent-boy to help us celebrate my 40th birthday. I learned later that they had phoned Bobby and asked him my most favorite type. I never realized I had one. I always thought of myself as pan-homo. That's one of the reasons I love living in New York City, because it has beautiful people from all over the world. In fact, it occurred to me recently that of the men I pass on the street wherever I might be in an average day, half of them are positively edible. And of the other half, half of *them* have some feature or quality that's endearing in some way or other, so I'd gladly take them on as well. So that leaves only a 25% reject list for all of New York City's ambulatory adult males!

Bobby told our friends that my favorite type is Latin, so they hired a cute Latino guy named Jason. He was very sweet and hot and a good sport. We had a fun (safe) romp, and then Jason stayed around for a glass of wine, and a kiss, and a few chaste pictures (to send to our benefactors). It felt like the old days. Not having a professional in for sex—we had never done that before—but having a light-hearted encounter in our bed that was free of emotional baggage. *That's it*, I think. It wasn't that I wanted more sex in my life, but that I craved lightness and freedom. Easiness. Simplicity. And without it, I began to shut down.

Isn't libido a strange phenomenon? The most powerful of drives at times, and yet the first to go. I always thought. If I don't feel well, I'll say no to the most glorious cock on Earth. If I'm very hungry, or very thirsty, count me out of the orgy until those drives are sated. If I've had a sudden fright—or loss—then the most beautiful limbs, the softest skin, the most pheromonic scent, the most exquisite ass, the warmest smile, the most gloriously sculpted chest, the handsomest hands, the sweetest breath, the most eager kiss, the best of maleness is wasted on me. Until I've had time to recover, of course.

I felt that Bobby and I were on a downward trajectory. And I couldn't seem to find a way to turn it around. And yet, it was now normal. And we lived it, one day at a time.

# Chapter Three

**By the summer of 1991**, Bobby was not the only one in iffy shape. Depressed, I think, is how I'd describe my condition. The years of waiting and watching had taken their toll. Not to mention the elbow-bending, as Bobby used to call it. I was only teaching the occasional class, here and there. My catering business was not going anywhere, without my constant attention. And my cookbooks were not earning much, either.

A friend told me about a drug study at the big facility—university medical center and New York State something-or-other—at 168th Street and the Hudson. I went for an interview and was accepted. This particular study was testing the effectiveness of an old-fashioned antidepressant (which doctors rarely prescribed anymore) when used to treat alcoholism. It was a double blind test, so there was no way of knowing whether or not I would be taking the actual drug. It was the medical care and the counseling I wanted. I had done talk therapy once before, when I was a graduate student. I believed in it. And it was all free.

Kathleen Hoolihan was the friend who recommended the study. She moved to New York from Dublin decades before and was a flight attendant with a major airline. Kathy flew all over the world—with gusto—and collected friends wherever she went.

She loved to cook and started assisting classes at the culinary center. So that's how we met. And we had been close for a decade.

Kathy's native mental health was buoyant, indeed. But of course, years of heavy drinking take their toll. Kathy was pleased to learn that I was accepted and had started the program. She had been through it herself, and she was happy I was assigned the same counselor. "You'll love Rudy. Say hi for me. I always remember he said to me, 'You're the most outgoing depressed person I've ever met.'" And so she was.

It was at the same time, I think, that I started going to the gym. It was a new experience. I hadn't been in a locker room since college, where "fitness training" meant "Let's see how long you can run before you throw up." No, the YMCA was something else entirely. It was about adults who showed up because they wanted to, because they cared about health, strength, and beauty. Much to my surprise, I fell in love with the practice of exercise.

Bobby had always done his exercises at home. He had a strict regimen. I needed the community to pull me into the process. And I landed right where I needed to be. The ritual of showing up at the YMCA and heading down to the locker room also had a spiritual component. For those three hours, devoted (mostly) to fitness, I never had the slightest craving for a cigarette, or a martini for that matter. Even the thought of my vices would have sullied the purity of the meditation.

This was new territory. I explored it greedily.

As we moved into fall, Bobby took a two-week gig in Toronto. I didn't mind all that much being alone. It helped me to focus on getting sober and getting fit. And Scooter was excellent company. Life went on.

Bobby's old friend Geoff was one of the very few people we saw that year. His partner Ronald had died the spring before. It was terrible to watch Ronald's health decline. He had been so pretty and lively, and then it all started to slip away. You may remember I told you that I visited him shortly before his death and found him dangerously lean and covered with herpes and medication. It was obvious to me—if not to Geoff—that the end was very near.

Geoff had been buoyed by deep denial throughout Ronald's decline. And even when Ronald died, Geoff seemed his usual, self-possessed self. One afternoon I got a phone call from James Tree, everyone's favorite leading lady. Geoff had "discovered" him when James first started working in New York, right out of college. In those early days he had not gotten into drag yet, but instead James was doing these weird and lovely monologues where he transformed his face and body into those of some wistful, tortured creature. Usually female.

I knew James from university. He was a freshman when I was a graduate student, and I actually did a play with him once. So when Geoff asked us to go with him to a funny little theater downtown to see the budding talent he had discovered, we were happy to join him. Geoff and James became close friends over the years, and James never forgot Geoff's support in his early career.

We met for coffee on the West Side. "I'm worried about Geoffrey," James said. "Ever since Ronald got sick, he's been living in some alternate reality. Look who's talking! I know you and Bobby have known him for a very long time."

"He and Bobby have been close for twenty years. But, Jimmy, what can we do?" I asked.

"I don't know. But if he doesn't accept Ronald's death and mourn the loss, then I think he'll crack up. You see him, don't you?"

"Yes, every other week or so."

"Well, please keep an eye on him. He's a precious man, and I'd hate to lose him," James said.

"Yes, of course, Jimmy," I said. "And I'll keep in touch." I was concerned about Geoff, but I didn't have the heart to tell James I was even more concerned about *my own* precious man that I'd hate to lose. And I sensed that I *was* losing him.

One evening, late summer, when Geoff came to supper, he was his usual jocular self, even as he told me that Dr. Foscari had died. Steve Foscari was the controversial young doctor who invented a treatment regimen for AIDS victims, a treatment he once thought might be right for me. And now I learned that he had treated Ronald, and himself, of course, and hadn't been able to save either of them.

Geoff seemed almost cheerful. I was deeply disturbed, both by his demeanor and his news. But after that, Geoff seemed to go into a slide. And by fall we were entertaining an alcoholic shadow of our friend. He still came to dinner occasionally. Bobby was fiercely loyal, even in his impaired state. The two of them could sit together for hours, drinking and enjoying an old friendship that required no pretense.

I began to think more about myself and less about Bobby and his world. That was it, I think. That was the transition.

For the last few years we had taken most of our suppers, when we were alone, on bed trays in front of the television. I liked it. It was cozy. It was our ritual. But that fall, as I grew soberer, I began to feel a drive toward getting things done. I wanted to go to the computer after dinner and write recipes for my classes, and such. And I just couldn't seem to do it after settling into bed for supper. There is something to be said, after all, for keeping bed for sleeping, alone—conditioning the brain to react in an accustomed way to various venues.

I decided to start serving dinner, when we were alone (which was most of the time, now) on the dining-room table. It felt like the right thing to do. I wanted to be productive. I wanted to energize my existence and my career. "We've been having dinner in the bedroom for years," Bobby said. "You can't just change things just like that."

"Oh yeah, watch me!" I hope I didn't really say that. But surely I said something like it, and the results were not good. In the weeks that followed, dinner conversation was icy at best. I don't even remember how the bed tray/dining table standoff played out. Maybe we went back to bed trays, at least a few nights a week. I can't bear to think too much more about it.

But the important thing is that Bobby sensed a change in me, as I gradually sobered. He was not

happy about it—how many of us are really comfortable with change?—and he wanted to blame it on the
drug I was taking (which turned out to be the pla-
cebo, by the way). It was just one more negativity in
his life, and he didn't need more. But I provided it
anyway. Because it seemed my only possible path.
At the time. Now? Like every other situation in life,
I'm sure I might have handled it better.

One night I had a blinding headache and no
drugs to fight it. I don't make that mistake these
days, but back then I was sometimes caught unpre-
pared. I got out of bed and went to the dining room
to sit and try to figure out a strategy for dealing with
the pain. Should I take a belt of Scotch? Probably
not. Bobby hadn't conked out yet—so it must have
been fairly early in the fall—so he came out to ex-
press sympathy, of course. But he also questioned
my therapy. He had no confidence in my doctors or
the program I had joined. He wanted the headache
to be a product of the drug I was (not) taking, because it had upset his life.

Naturally, my head throbbed all the more as I
countered his arguments. And I still had to figure
out how to get through the next few hours. I decided
on hydrotherapy—the only non-narcotic treatment
for migraine I've ever discovered: I got into the
shower and let hot water pelt my head and neck, di-
aling up the water until it was hotter than I thought
I could actually stand. And then I waited. It can feel
like hours. Who knows for sure how long it takes?
But eventually the heat induces a fever that breaks
the headache. That's how it feels to me. More and
more heat until it *breaks*.

Weak-as-a-kitten is the aftermath, though why
it's called that I couldn't say; kittens I've known have

been ferociously strong.  But at least the searing pain is gone.  And sleep becomes a blessed possibility.  I treated myself.  I was doing the best I could.  It was all I could manage.  I was sobering up.

# Chapter Four

**In December, our holiday joy** was muted to say the least. I don't even remember whether I decorated a tree or not. Counseling, gym, and the rare class to teach. That was my reality. I think it was right around Christmas that I answered the phone one afternoon and took a message for Bobby, which I delivered as soon as he got home. He had been to a photo shoot for a magazine article about cabaret in New York. His eyes were so bloodshot that morning that we tried everything to clear them, for the camera—blue eye drops from Canada, witch hazel. Nothing seemed to work. I didn't even want to know how the pictures would turn out.

"You got a call about an hour ago," I said, as he walked in. "Charles Digby, from Toronto. I wrote down his number."

"Thanks," he said and headed for the bathroom. I was playing with Scooter when Bobby came out of the bathroom and sat on the edge of the bed. He had been crying. And then he confessed that he had an affair in Toronto during his last job there. He was horribly ashamed and contrite.

My reaction was muted, as in most situations in my life those days. Was I deeply wounded? No. A few years before, Bobby's admission of a deliberate infidelity would have been devastating. But we had come to the point where I was uncertain whether I

really cared or not.  And the worst of it was that es-
sentially, Bobby wanted it to be my fault!  Like
everything else that had gone wrong in our lives.  I
wasn't supporting him.  I wasn't giving him what he
needed, physically and emotionally.  And so, of
course, he acted out.

I registered Bobby's considerable pain around the
incident and everything that surrounded it.  But I
was unwilling to assume the burden of additional
blame.  And so I pretty much let go of it and got on
with my routine.  I was unwilling to be de-railed, that
season.  And so I kept to my course.

📖

And then came the tearful admission that Friday
morning in late January that Bobby had refilled his
medication and swallowed it all, hoping to be dead
by morning.  Instead, he was very much alive and in
even more emotional pain than before.  I resolved to
get him medical care as soon as possible.  There was
only one hitch:  I was scheduled to teach a class in
New Jersey that evening.  I had neglected my career
so much that this class was one of my only professional commitments for the month.

My first instinct was to go to New Jersey and
teach as scheduled.  I had a nagging feeling that
Bobby had planned this event—subconsciously, no
doubt—for a day when it would have maximum im-
pact.  And my sense of self-preservation was piqued
by it.  I was able to get my counselor Rudy on the
phone.  The program had just ended that week, so I
was on my own.  But Rudy took my call.  It would be
the last one, but at least I had that last call.  I

explained the situation, and said, "I think I should go ahead and teach."

"I think you're absolutely right," Rudy said. That affirmation was precious to me. And I sprang into action: I got Kathy on the phone. She had just flown in from God-knows-where and desperately needed sleep. "Sorry to do this to you, Sweetie," I said, "but Bobby's in really bad shape. He needs to go to Emergency, but I can't take him. I've got to show up and teach in New Jersey. The class was scheduled last year, and I can't just back out. But Bobby shouldn't be alone. Can you come over?"

"Of course," she said. "Just give me an hour."

"Bless you," I said and hung up.

I had qualms about calling Kathy. Sides had been taken the past year. And our friendship felt strained. But I didn't know where else to turn. I knew she adored Bobby, that he reminded her of her father—also a musician. So, while I no longer trusted her entirely with our friendship, I knew she would come through for Bobby. And she did.

The tension was palpable, but I proceeded to shave and shower and gather my equipment. Kathy arrived. "New York Hospital is just up Sutton Place, you know. It's only a ten minute walk," I told her. "Emergency is around the corner from the main building. Easy to find. I'll get home as soon as I can, and if you're not here I'll walk up and find you." Cell phones were scarce in those days. Communication was tricky. I went on autopilot. I headed for Port Authority and the bus to Tenafly.

Once at the school, I put on my professional hat and got on with it. The class went well. I was in good form. The students seemed pleased, and the food we produced was delicious. Then we cleaned up in

29

record time, and the owners drove me home. At night, it's a twenty-minute drive. During the day, try to get across the George Washington Bridge in twenty minutes!

I had no idea what I would find when I let myself into the apartment and greeted Scooter. Nobody? Kathy alone after she had returned from the hospital? Instead I found Bobby and Kathy having a nightcap."

"What did they say?" I asked.

"We didn't go," Kathy said.

"What do you mean, you didn't go?" I asked, or rather demanded.

"Bobby didn't want to go to Emergency, so we went to dinner instead," Kathy said.

And who knows how many drinks they had with dinner. I was horrified. "How could you?" I hope I didn't shriek. "You know Bobby needs help!"

"I can't force Bobby to do something he doesn't want to do, and, besides, where were you?" she said. The recriminations flew back and forth for a bit, and then Kathy went home. I was relieved to have my old friend out of my home and out of my sight.

Bobby was subdued. There didn't seem to be much else to do that night, so I gave Scooter a walk, and then we all turned in. Did I sleep that night? Not really. Bobby and Scooter both seemed to sleep like babies. I listened to a lot of breathing. And a little snoring, from both of them. Proof of life. But eventually, of course, that night was over.

The next morning, we got up and had coffee and a bite of Saturday breakfast, as usual. The day was tense but uneventful, except that just as we were headed out to a neighborhood pub for a bite of supper—pork chops and fish-and-chips, that sort of thing—Bobby got a phone call from Beverly Hills from his best friend from high school. Hollywood High, that is.

"Hi, Bobby. It's Arlene. Sorry to tell you this, but I thought you'd want to know that Emma died today." Her firstborn had suffered an overdose, or committed suicide, or both. "Keith and I are broken up about it, of course. I won't stay on the phone."

"No, of course not, but thanks for letting me know. Much love to you both. I'll call you in a few days. Hang in there." That sort of thing. And then we headed out to the pub. We got through our supper without incident, but then after dinner—and after another vodka—Bobby began to weep with grief and empathy for Arlene and Keith. I don't know whether I sensed an opening, or what, but I suggested—firmly—that we go to Emergency at New York Hospital. And he agreed. I wasted no time paying the check and getting us out the door and into a taxi.

As we waited at Emergency, Bobby suggested that it was not necessary and that we should go home. I was firm. It felt like an eternity, but it was probably not more than thirty minutes before the on-duty shrink appeared to interview Bobby. He was gentle and professional. I didn't envy him his job.

Bobby explained that two days earlier he had attempted an overdose that failed to kill him and that now he was overcome with grief for a friend's misfortune. The doctor asked a number of questions for clarification, and finally, the big question: "If we send you home tonight, will you try it again?"

"Yes," Bobby said. And that proved to be the magic answer. In that moment, with that reply, he became a ward of the state. He would be assigned to a mental health facility, as directed by hospital policy, the City of New York, and the State of New York. Maybe the fucking federal government, too, I don't know. But at that instant, Bobby's survival was no longer my sole responsibility. For the first time in sixteen years.

The next minutes were tense, of course, as the hospital staff figured out what to do with him. Calls were made to various hospitals. Bobby's medical insurance had lapsed—as had so much of the responsible behavior in our lives—so placing him was tricky. And in the end, New York Hospital was forced to admit Bobby to their own Payne Whitney clinic. It was highly regarded. And it was next door.

It was only later that I chuckled at the irony of the situation—that Bobby knew the Paynes and the Whitneys, and now he was being sheltered in the facility that some of them had endowed. But that night, I was concerned only with seeing Bobby in some safe place. It was time for me to leave, so I embraced him, of course, and kissed him, of course, and promised him that I would see him in the morning. And then they led him away.

I made my way out of the hospital complex to York Avenue. Can I say that it was as if a great weight had been lifted from my shoulders? Yes. But I was also horrified that our lives had reached that point. And I was terrified about the future. It was nearly midnight when I got home. It was hardly more than a ten-minute walk from the hospital, but the winter air that had first been such a relief after hours in the hospital hothouse soon started to chill me to the core. I was shivering uncontrollably when I let myself into the dark apartment.

Scooter came bounding from the bedroom to greet me, just as if it were a normal night. As soon as I got some lights on and greeted Scooter properly, I took off my coat and headed for the kitchen. I pushed up my sleeves, and ran warm water over my hands and wrists. Soon my body temperature normalized, but it took a while for the shivers to abate.

With some sense of normality restored, I was free to contemplate the situation. On the one hand, there was a profound sense of relief. For the first time in two years I was not on suicide watch. Bobby's very survival was not my immediate responsibility. The freedom of it might have been exhilarating but for the fact that—on the other hand—I felt desperately lonely. And terrified.

I bundled up again and took Scooter for a quick walk. He was grateful for the attention after a quiet evening alone. I wasn't up for the long version, but Scooter got some exercise and I got a bit more fresh air. The quiet of the city late at night and the view across the East River always have a calming effect on me. Even that weird night. When we got back to the apartment, Scooter got his little treats—each one carefully balanced on his nose until the clap that signaled it was time for him to flip and catch. Nearly normal, I noted.

I switched on the radiator in the bedroom for a few minutes, to take off the chill. We didn't use it much because the thermostat was unreliable. But I sensed that I would need a little comfort. Nights with Bobby that last year had become increasingly fitful:

His sleep was restless, and his body would release a huge amount of heat in the middle of the night, signaling the effects of advanced alcoholism.

I never turned on the TV that night. I hadn't gotten ready for bed without television for countless years. Maybe I didn't want any distractions from the situation. Maybe I just thought the electronic babysitter was an inappropriate crutch. Over at Payne Whitney, they were certainly not tucking Bobby in with the Late Show. I wanted normality, but I didn't want to miss anything. I didn't want to medicate, to dodge reality in any way.

As I brushed my teeth, I wondered how I would get through the next few days. How long would Bobby be hospitalized? What would be expected of me? How would I take care of myself? I also wondered if I might get a really good night's sleep, for a change. But alone is alone, after all. And alone was never my best suit.

I nearly invited Scooter up onto the bed to sleep with me. But Bobby and I had decided years before that was a bad idea. No, I was not going to do something stupid and break a decade of tradition. Good, solid, healthy tradition. No. And yet my brain was spinning with fears and fantasies. But I was exhausted, and I conked out almost as soon as my head hit the pillow.

# Chapter Five

**The staff was very kind to me**, I must say. I was obviously the next of kin in this situation, and no one questioned it. I've felt that same acceptance in other situations through the years, in New York City hospitals, that is. I've been spared the horror of being denied access to a patient because I lack blood credentials. That kind of exclusion was standard in the years before Marriage. Especially in other cities, I'm told. Mercifully, it never happened to me.

In the morning a doctor evaluated Bobby. They had already started him on a Librium detox program—just enough drug to calm the withdrawal symptoms. How long would it take? No one could say for sure. Bobby was conscious and fairly rational, but mostly he just sat and shook. I didn't know whether his nerves were shot or he was processing the overdose of thyroid medication. The doctor didn't seem to know, either.

Bobby and I talked a little, about trivial things, but mostly we just sat. I held his hand. The shaking was alarming. I ignored it. I stayed with him for most of the day. We sat in his room for hours, but I also accompanied him to the little dining hall on his floor for meals. I probably fed him, that first day, anyway. I can't quite remember. I know I gave him a shave early on that week. It wasn't too close—I couldn't bring myself to guide the razor upward against the grain, as he always did, and as I always did on my own face. After decades of shaving—starting with those bizarre contraptions called "safety razors," which are scarcely safer than straight razors, if at all—I just couldn't shave Bobby's face the same way I would my own. It felt too dangerous. But at least I got him cleaned up a bit.

I recall some of his fellow inmates, the crazier ones. And a sweet young man who seemed quite lost. It was not fun. Bobby's doctor took me aside to say, "You're going to need some help, too. I suggest you start attending meetings of [the famous 12-Step program that was founded by the wives of alcoholics]. In New York there are meetings every day all over the city. I think the nurses' station might have a schedule, if you need it. You owe it to yourself to give it a try." I would hear that same advice from other sources in the next few days. I had no intention of fighting it. I went. Often. I went to see Bobby every morning, and then I went to a meeting.

As any member will tell you, I went to get help for Bobby and stayed to get help for me. At first I couldn't figure out why all these people were sharing about *their* feelings and *their* recovery, while I was desperate to understand *Bobby's* situation. But as an adjunct to the work at hand—my recovery—I was also able to get a little advice after meetings from members who had been through similar situations. And that's how I learned what to expect during Bobby's detox. And how I learned that rehab was next.

How on earth was that going to happen? Who was going to pay for a twenty-eight-day rehab program? And if Bobby didn't go, then how would I care for him at home? There was just enough money in the checking account to cover the rent for a few months.  And a little food, as long as I didn't eat too much.  Did I decide to trust in my Higher Power and turn it over?  Not really.  I couldn't get to the let-go-and-let-God stage.  Never have, entirely.  But I did manage to "hang on loose," and let the Universe do its thing.

Without complete surrender, somehow I did learn to trust in the rightness of the moment.  Not Polly-anna bullshit about how everything happens for the best.  Just a sense that things are unfolding exactly as they should, whether I get it or not.  For example: One afternoon there was a phone call from a man I didn't know.  Well, he sounded like a man, but since I never actually met him, I have always assumed he was most likely an angel.  The voice explained that he knew some people at a top rehab facility in Min-neapolis (then the rehab capital of America).  He had arranged to have Bobby admitted—with no insur-ance and no financial guarantor.  Or maybe the angel guaranteed payment.  Who knows?

Everything was scheduled:  Bobby would be walked from his room at Payne Whitney to a waiting cab that would transport him to La Guardia for the flight to Minneapolis, where he would be met by a rehab person and escorted to the facility.  Neat.  It seemed too good to be true, and yet it all came off without a hitch.  How relieved was I?

The first month—when Bobby was in the Payne Whitney lockup—was fraught, of course.  So many new experiences.  So much to figure out.  Part of every day with Bobby, and part of every day devoted to self-care.  It really did last a solid month.  Bobby was in such bad shape that he truly needed three weeks of detox.  The fourth week they were trying to figure out what to do with him. And then came the angel intervention.

By the beginning of that second month, I had learned to cherish my freedom. I swore I would use every moment—as long as our meager funds lasted—to focus only on healing and growth. When the call came inviting me to "family week" in Minneapolis, I was at first inclined to decline. I didn't want to go! But I spoke to someone, after a meeting, who had been there, and she assured me, "It's not for him, it's for you. Anything you want to say to him, you have to say it there. And he will be forced to listen. And if you don't go and say it, then forget it. He'll never be able to hear it again in the same way."

Well, I'm not stupid, so I started making travel plans. Once again, doors opened. The rehab center got me a cheap flight and recommended a hotel that would book me without a credit card as backup. So I was not the only family member whose cards were all canceled during the race to the bottom. I still didn't want to go—and give up a week of freedom—but I was resigned. And resolved. And I began to write my story for Bobby to hear.

Now, Bobby was part of a group of ten or twelve men who all bonded in their first two weeks together. I met them. Some were delightful, and some were troubled. But they all knew why they were there. Their families? Not so much. Deep in the State of Denial, some of us were. And some of us were deep into anger and other negativities. But I remember a couple from Montana who had been divorced for many years, and yet they came together to support their son. I will never forget their devotion to the common cause. And as a result, I now believe that

Montana actually exists, while before it had always seemed a fantasy state in my consciousness.

We family members went to counseling sessions and meetings together. It was all good. And then came the big day when we gathered in a room that was large enough to accommodate patients lined up in front and family seated like an audience. The moderator opened the meeting as a Meeting. And when they went down the line introducing themselves, I heard Bobby say, "Hi, I'm Bobby, and I'm an alcoholic."

I felt a deep little death in the bottom of my heart. Why? Partly because he seemed so cowed by it. No. I must be honest. *He* seemed resigned. *I* felt cowed by it. Because it felt like a negation of our lives together. As much as I respected his journey, and as much as I had yearned for sobriety in our relationship, that simple admission seemed to put the last sixteen years into question: Did Bobby really love me, or was it just vodka? Had we built a beautiful shared life, or was it just vodka? Had we soared together to the heights of love and friendship, or was it just vodka? Had I pinned my very existence to a wonderful dream of unity, or was it just vodka?

I didn't have much time to contemplate, because I was soon called to the "witness chair" to testify. I took out my notes and opened both barrels. I told Bobby everything I wanted him to hear about how his drinking had affected his life and his career, and, of course, mine. I even talked about how the last year had numbed me sexually. I even stated that I made it a point to get myself up and off about once a week, just to be sure I was still alive. I'm working purely from memory, here. I didn't save my script; or if I did, I have no idea where it is. Fortunately.

It was draining. You could have heard a pin drop in the room. I said everything I needed to say. Everything I wanted him to hear. And he heard it. And so did everyone else. At dinner the next evening—I think they let Bobby go off-campus with me—he told me that one of the guys in his group had *his* family week coming up the following week, and no family to attend. And another guy said to him, "Don't worry! I called Bobby's mate, and he said he'd be happy to come back and do *your* family week!"

I laughed, in spite of myself. It was good to laugh. It felt so like real life. And yet what would real life look like now, I wondered. And how, from where we started, could we possibly have ended up in this steak house in Minneapolis? One day at a time, I suppose.

# Chapter Six

**When Bobby returned** from Minneapolis, we began to navigate our new relationship. I tried to be supportive. I also tried to be independent. It was a balancing act. Bobby was just where he was supposed to be: sober, cautious, and willing to attend meetings. He even got invitations from some of New York's A-list former drunks. Word gets around quickly in Celebrity Land. Two or three of them I would have been keen to meet, but this was emphatically not about me.

Program talks about spiritual damage being the last to heal. I could see it. Bobby was in good shape physically. He was working, now and then. He was attending meetings. He was sober. But with all his healing, he still had some "stinkin' thinkin' " going on. Negativity, principally. Sadness, around the edges. And I never figured out exactly how much of the past Bobby truly took responsibility for. And that meant someone else was responsible for the rest. And that someone, of course, was me.

But there was more going on, of course, than a new sobriety. As much as I was all about going to the gym and going to meetings and trying to repair my life and my career, there was also a new sense that I should be doing all of this on my own. I don't think there was a Road to Damascus moment. It was months into my counseling and tapering off booze before I had any sense of where we were headed. I can't identify the moment I first entertained the notion that I had the right to end the relationship: the right to make a choice for my life that did not include Bobby—as if any choice in my life could ever not include Bobby.

Not so mysterious, really. Don't the majority of alcoholic relationships fail? But our relationship was different, wasn't it? And it was supposed to be forever. So I was faced with a situation where, on the one hand, a break was an absolute necessity, and on the other hand, the idea of that break was breaking my heart. But like so much that year, I showed up and walked through it.

📖

So, how did I tell Bobby? I didn't, really, and I'll always be deeply ashamed of how it played out: In late June I attended the Pride march with a gym friend. And in the course of the afternoon we encountered an actor friend of Bobby's who was enjoying the festivities with a group of friends. We hung out with them for a while. Len asked after Bobby, of course. I hadn't really discussed the situation with anyone outside of Program. But it felt good to open up a bit. I must have told him that it looked as though we were planning to separate.

The next afternoon, when I returned home from my morning errands, Bobby called me into the bedroom and said, "Listen to this."

"This" was a voice message on our answering machine. It went something like this: "Hi, I'm Linda, and I'm a friend of Len's. He told me you're looking for an apartment, and I may know something that would work for you. If you're interested, call me back at 555-6709."

I was as shocked as Bobby was. My first instinct was to lie. That's unusual for me. Normally, under pressure, I suffer from an excess of truth. But I dissembled. "I never told Len I was looking for an apartment," or something equally lame with a kernel of truth in it. But the cat was out of that bag. And we could no longer pretend that everything was going to be all right.

In the next week, plans were made. Bobby decided to move out. I decided to keep the apartment. Affordable rent-stabilized two-bedroom, two-bathroom apartments just off Sutton Place were rare, then as now. I calculated the amount of roommate rent I could demand, and decided I could pull it off. Bobby found a studio sublet across the street, as it happened. And I took out the lease-renewal form, which was due immediately.

Both of our names were on the lease, fortunately. With shaking hands, I selected the two-year renewal, wrote a check for the security deposit increase, and requested that the management company renew in my name only, removing Bobby's. I was terrified, but I walked through it and then delivered the renewal form myself to the management office. The receptionist, who had always been unpleasant, was her usual acerbic self. She refused to write me a receipt for the delivery. I was as pleasant as possible, but also firm. And eventually we arrived at some sort of compromise. I left the office with a dated document that could prove—I hoped—that I had submitted the form before the deadline.

Vacancy rent increases were quite juicy in those days. And the management company was famously unscrupulous. Every precaution had to be taken to assure they could not possibly take action to evict. Recent changes in the law guaranteed that tenants had the right to one roommate. I had been very careful, and yet I was still fearful. For another month. But then it worked out: My copy of the renewal was eventually forwarded with the management signature. And they crossed out Bobby's name!

The rest of the summer was mostly about handling the separation details. One day, though, I put all of that on hold and attended Lanny Kirk's memorial. Lanny had grown increasingly sick that year. I took him some food, twice I think. I had far too much experience, from the previous decade, of cooking for AIDS victims. I know I made my usual rice pudding with lots of cream and a little butter worked in. A little extra-good vanilla. I wanted it to be irresistible, even to a weakened appetite.

The second time I showed up at the famous apartment on Horatio Street, Rob was out and Lanny was in bad shape. He opened the door just a crack, reluctantly accepted my gift, and closed the door again. Did he need my rice pudding and oatmeal cookies? Obviously not. What he needed was health. And that was beyond me. Did I suspect I'd never see him again? Probably.

The memorial was held in a large theater. There must have been at least a thousand people in the audience. And many speakers, too. The most touching tribute to Lanny came from his Broadway costar from forty years earlier. They had maintained their friendship through the years, and had even shared a cabaret bill the year before, atop the RCA Building at Rockefeller Center. I think those were Lanny's last performances. She said something like this: "Of all the men in my life [and we all knew that included her famous husband, whom she had married twice] Lanny is the only one who's loved me deeply, simply, tenderly, and completely."

I don't know what I'd have said, if I had been asked to speak. Which I was not. But I adored Lanny, and I felt very proud that he had once offered me friendship. Rob was there, of course. We spoke briefly and hugged, of course. I thought he seemed a bit lost, but just as charming as ever. I began to wonder about *his* health. Surely he was Positive, too. Rob looked almost fit enough, but not quite the same as the robust beauty I had flirted with just two years before. Bobby didn't come with me to the memorial. He was working, luckily. I was glad to be alone. And it was good practice for the future.

By August, things were falling into place. Bobby planned his move for September 1. I found a gay meeting I liked very much and made a few new near-friends. And among them I lined up some helpers for the clean-up-paint-up-fix-up that would follow Bobby's move. And then it came time to "divide up the things."

Who gets the teapot from Fortnum & Mason? Who gets the love seat? Who gets which electronics?

Bobby knew how to travel light, more or less. He asked for things he needed, things that had been his before our relationship and that would still be useful to him in his new life, and just a very few things from our years together that he couldn't bear to part with. I got the Christmas ornaments and Scooter. We had not even one dispute. If he said, "I'd like to take this," then I said, "Of course." And if I said, "I'd like to keep this," then he said, "Of course."

And that's how we did it. Very civilized. Blood-less, almost. It had to be done. We did it. And nothing was ever the same, of course. How could it be? Even though Bobby was recovered enough to get on with his life again, he had a sense of loss about him. Or did I imagine it? An autumnal quality that had never really been there before. I think I kicked him in the gut and left a fissure that never quite healed as it should. I only say that because I felt I had been kicked in the chest, and my heart would never quite heal.

He never saw it coming. Nor did I, really. I never told him how painful the split was for me. After all those years of telling him everything, I retreated to another place to lick my wounds and try to emerge healed and whole on the other side. *I never told him.* How could I? How could I possibly tell the love of my life that our love had become toxic? That was the reality of it: I feared I'd die if I stayed in our life to-gether. And I feared that Bobby was okay with that. I sensed that his own death was . . .not a light thing, but a possibility he could embrace. I was unwilling to go there with him.

After all our joyous journeys together, I saw our paths diverge. And it chilled my soul right to the marrow (to borrow from a Carole King song). But a wee, small voice in my heart spoke to me about the future. And I would not go down for the count. No. Not me. No. I had hopes, and dreams, and a lust for life—and lust—that had only just been blunted by the alcoholic stupor that pushed Bobby to the bottom. I was not ready to surrender to the dark side. I chose life.

## Chapter Seven

**At the end of August 1992** we learned that our acquaintance, Hank, had lost his mate to the Epidemic. I knew boys were still dying, of course. I had attended Lanny's memorial just the month before. Perhaps it had become so normal that I scarcely noticed as long as the dead boy was not a friend. Or a friend of a friend, as in this case. But as my last official act as social secretary for the partnership, I wrote Hank a condolence note. And then Bobby moved out September 1.

Moving day is never pretty, I think. But when it's about new beginnings, then some of the sting might be lifted. I wasn't certain what I was feeling about the whole thing. What had I ever been all that certain of, except that I always knew I loved Bobby? And now?

We ferried most of Bobby's stuff across the street ourselves. But of course it would take piano movers to handle the Steinway. They were pleasant enough until they suggested—firmly—that Bobby pay an additional $100 for insurance. In case they dropped the thing. It made no sense. Surely a safe move should be included in any contract. It felt like extortion, but Bobby paid the money, and off they went. And they didn't drop it. They even got it in through the service entrance, without having to hoist it up the front façade and into an opening where a big window would have been removed.

Geoff came over to help Bobby move, more or less. He was mostly a drunken shell of his former self at that point. Bobby was so kind to him that I might have been more sympathetic, had it been an easier day. Geoff seemed only about fifty percent present. And his face had lost *more* than fifty percent of its youthful beauty. It isn't that we love our friends for their beauty, of course. We really love them for their faults. But we rejoice in their beauty as a part of who they are. And when it fades—as it always does—then we continue to celebrate the traces, the reminders of past splendors. Yes, human beauty is heartbreaking—for the beholder and for the holder as well.

When that day finally ended, Scooter and I were alone in the apartment. It seemed so empty. And compared to the day before, indeed it was empty. Seventeen years of cohabitation, most of it joyous. And it was suddenly over. I never wallowed in it. There was too much work to do. And no time for self-pity.

We were new neighbors, after all, and there were two nights I slept over at Bobby's new apartment while the building was redoing the floors in what was now "mine," rather than "ours." It was so painful for me, sleeping with Bobby without touching him. I can't imagine that it was much easier for him. Even Scooter seemed uneasy with the arrangement. Bobby told me later that Scooter started scratching at the front door as soon as I left to go and investigate the progress on the flooring across the street. We decided that would be the last of Scooter's visits to Bobby's new place. It had that same finality about it as did the breakup.

The next week, he invited me to a little supper get-together with my friend Kathy. I can't say exactly why I went, but I realized instantly that it was a mistake. Sides had been taken, and the sense of betrayal was keen. In fact, I didn't see Kathy again until—never mind. Perhaps I'll be able to tell you about it later, but not now.

And in another week or so, Bobby invited me to join some friends—mine, originally, and now ours—who had been very supportive of him during the breakup. Supportive of me? Not so much, I thought. They had him over for dinner—to help him over the rough patch—and now he was returning the favor. I declined the invitation as cheerfully as possible. It felt like a minefield best avoided.

I had to scramble to get the apartment ready to receive a roommate. The second bedroom had been my office for years. Out came all the books and files, the desk, the computer, and the printer. All of that had to go into my room, while the bed and some odds and ends of furniture went into the back room. It was not pretty, exactly, but it was serviceable. There were even rugs. And I installed a long mirror on the inside of the bedroom door. The tub in the hall bathroom had long been used for storage. I had to remove all of that and revive the plumbing. There

was enough bed and bath linen to support a small
army.

A friend gave me a platform bed for my room. *My
room*, indeed. It had been *our room* for nearly seventeen years.   It took some time to make the
adjustment.   But there was at least a low-level ex-
citement about starting afresh.

The loan I got from my parents bought me precious little time.  The first roommate who agreed to
my terms was bat-shit crazy. I knew it.  But I had a
financial deadline for getting the room rented.  And I
didn't realize quite how dangerous she was.  Had I
known that she would threaten not to pay the next
month's rent, and then disappear—and then haul
me into Housing Court—I would never have accepted
her deposit.  There was an angel who intervened on
my behalf, as there so often is in life.  A neighbor.
Catherine was a pretty young woman—on the soft
side of Texas blond—who lived two doors away with
her handsome young fiancé.

I didn't really know Catherine all that well, but
she knew about the drama and the changes in my
life.   And for some reason she offered to come to
Housing Court with me.  I was grateful for the support, of course.  When the judged ruled that not only
should I return the crazy's deposit but also her first
month's rent, and that I should do it within the next
half hour to avoid his sending the case across the
street to the criminal division, I was alarmed.  Naturally.

Catherine was much calmer than I was.  I think
she actually was from Texas, and I sensed she grew
up with privilege. And people with that kind of childhood are less fearful than the rest of us.  I think.  I
had the crazy's deposit with me—just in case.  But

the first month's rent?  Long since spent.  Catherine simply went to the nearest ATM, withdrew the sum, and handed it to me.  I handed it over to the crazy, got a receipt, and we were out of there.  There were a few psychotic jeers from the crazy as she did her victory dance.  But nothing Catherine and I couldn't handle.

"Pay me back when you can," Catherine said on our way home.  And I did.  Within the week.  Somehow.  "Don't fuck around with angels," someone said.  Surely *someone* said that.  Or should have.  Anyway, It's a motto of mine.

The roommate situation was sometimes quiet and sometimes all over the place.  Many of them stayed no more than a few months.  One was a young German guy working in publishing and trying his best to sort out his immigration and, therefore, employment situation.  He was forced to work for nothing.  The company had no intention of running afoul of the law, even though my roomie was listed on the magazine's masthead.  I hope they gave him some nice perks in exchange for free labor.  Even stupider than that was the trip outside the country he had to make every few months.  A quick visit to the German Consulate in Toronto or Juarez, Mex, would get his visa renewed for another few months.

One roommate was an actor, one was a fur saleswoman (at Famous East Side Department Store).  One was an insurance underwriter.  One of my favorites was an Australian woman about my age who was steeped in New Age wisdom.  Marcia had clients she did psychic readings for—sometimes in person and sometimes over the phone. And she could afford to pay the rent. That was always a plus.

# Chapter Eight

**I coped with loneliness** rather well, I think. I went to the gym and to meetings, lots of meetings. And in between time, I focused on the other most important requirements in my life: finding work and getting laid. Neither one was particularly easy. The work business, especially.

There were a few little job things that Program friends told me about. I spent nearly a month sitting at the little desk near the front door of a legendary designer and decorator's showroom on East 59th Street. There was absolutely nothing to do but smile at the dozen or so clients and colleagues who walked in the front door in the course of an average weekday. Not once did I have to direct anyone to the office manager or decorator they sought. They always knew where they were going.

Apparently there was some particularly valuable furniture in the front window. And that was my sole reason to be there. I had no security training. They just wanted a warm body wearing a tie up front to deter thieves. Since there was nothing to do, I thought, *What a gift! All this free time to read* The New York Times *and work on recipes for my next classes. And get paid, too!* But, of course, it doesn't really work that way.

Each morning, after greeting the staff and setting up my little desk with coffee and a snack (which I could easily hide and then sneak tastes of), I would carefully open my newspaper and settle in for a good read. But long before I had finished with the front page I would start to nod off. And then I had to drop the newspaper—or the recipe notes—and start practicing open-eye exercises. Anything to keep awake. A little walk out the front door, and then back again. Standing, sitting, standing again, pacing the little vestibule and studying the furniture I was meant to be guarding. It was torture, really. Totally humane, and yet torture none the less. Perhaps the worst of it was that I could have gotten so much more done on my own, and yet I was trapped there feeling so *unproductive*.

I also met some exceptionally creepy people in that industry—and that office. There was a cocktail party one evening that I was invited to. Not by the showroom manager—speaking of creepy people—but by my favorite salesman. Nice guy. Older. South American, as I remember. Very smart about the industry. A former associate at the most famous modern furniture company. Alejandro told me about the party and suggested I come. I put on a suit and showed up.

I hadn't attended anything that social in maybe two years. I wanted to see if I could still do it, without Bobby. Cocktail parties are all pretty much the same. Some more gala than others. Alejandro was there, of course, so I could always talk with him. He had a bit of a crush on me, so that made him supportive and courtly. I knew I looked good. I was thinner than ever before in my whole life. I was a decorative addition to the evening, actually. And every evening needs decorative additions.

Some of the guests were perfectly pleasant. The Old Man himself showed up and held court. He was almost never at the showroom during the work-day, but he was very much in evidence for the party. This was D & D, after all (Designers & Decorators), so it was an elegant crowd. I met a few fun people. Most of them seemed even more concerned with their own appearance than I was. But it was fine. And then I summoned my very best training in Knowing When to Leave and said my thank-yous and good-byes. Mostly to Alejandro and the showroom manager.

She was an icy little creature who had always been a bit unpleasant and condescending. But that evening as I thanked her for the party invite (even though it wasn't hers), she said something like, "I'm glad you were able to have this opportunity." My smile didn't waver, but as I headed home I said to myself, *That little cunt just said, "I'm glad you had this opportunity to mingle with your betters."* I was shocked, actually. I hadn't been dissed like that since high school, maybe. Or ever.

I know it sounds petty, but that kind of deliberate bad manners has always pulled me up short. I've seen it happen to others. If I belonged to another minority group, I'm sure I'd be more used to discrimination. If I were black or Jewish or even Polish, for that matter. "No Irish Need Apply" is not part of my experience, but I get it. In this case, we're talking about a woman whose very livelihood depended upon creative gay men. So this was certainly not a "No Faggots Allowed" situation. She just needed to feel that she was better than I am. And there's nothing you can do with people like that. I'm convinced.

That silly "job" ended on schedule, more or less. I had been asked to commit for the month, and then

the manager of the design building—who was my actual employer—told me that I was no longer needed
at the beginning of the fourth week. They were
changing the window, and that was that. It was awkward. Instead of just retreating, I decided to practice
a little self-care. I told the manager, clearly and
cleanly, that I was being treated unfairly, that I had
been engaged for one month, not three weeks.

She was unmoved by my story, but I'm guessing
she had a change of heart, or something, upon re-
flection. And my final check included payment for
that final week. Whatever her motive, it ended our
association on a positive note. Good business
karma, I'd say. The sum was a negligible part of her
budget, but very important to me at that moment.

I moved on. But before it was over, I was given
some beautiful fabric samples that I later used to
cover chair seats. And Alejandro took me to dinner
one night at a favorite little restaurant of his. He
came back to the apartment to see how I had managed to create a serious bookcase unit in the
entryway. Alejandro was sweet, but lacking in pas-
sion, I guess. So it wasn't going anywhere. But the
bookcase unit was solid.

📖

It would never have occurred to me to take a job
in a department store, except that I needed income.
And health insurance is certainly nice to have. So
when the director of the culinary center where I
taught called to tell me about an "opportunity," I
sprang into action. It was the famous East Side

department store, and it was only a ten-minute walk from the apartment.

The job seemed simple enough: organizing the cookware product demonstrations and doing some of them myself, plus—and this was the only part that really interested me—hosting live events with guest chefs.  Various manufacturers and shelter magazines scheduled occasional events, and I would be encouraged to develop my own.  That sounded like fun.

The pay was terrible, but at the high end of the salary range I might be able to pull it off.  When they made me an offer at the *bottom* of the salary range, I felt mildly insulted.  I was, after all, over-qualified.  I held out.  I was nervous, but determined not to undervalue my time. They countered with a mid-range offer, and I accepted.

Corporate America.  My, my.  I hadn't been near it since I was a supermarket produce clerk at age fifteen.  The learning curve was steep.  The worst of it was, the position was a union job; and so, the moment I was hired I became the enemy.  When I realized what was going on, I was glad I held out for an extra dollar an hour, because no raise would ever come from Corporate that had not been wrenched from them through collective bargaining.  The ugliness of it all was breathtaking.

And speaking of ugliness—call me sheltered, but I never thought to see human behavior like that of the young "executives."  I won't bore you with a full account.  But I have to mention that these children were vicious and ruthless.  Some of the things they said to career salespeople—who were, after all, the competent ones in this mix—would curl your hair.  "Do this.  Now.  Or I'll write you up and take you to personnel." That sort of thing. I was shocked. Like Vera in *Pal Joey*, "I've seen a lot. I mean, a lot." But nothing in my life had prepared me for the way these babies navigated their little orbits.

But I showed up for work five days a week—often on time—and did mostly what was expected of me. I also began to learn how to watch my back, which was always available for target practice. I never had to put on an elf costume, mercifully. But there were times when I might have been dressed as a clown for all the respect I felt.

But on the positive side of the ledger, I started making appointments with the doctors and dentists I had been avoiding in recent, insurance-less years. And I got very good at hosting cooking shows. The last year in particular I made some good contacts in the restaurant industry and even landed a tiny gig on the Food Network. So I guess I'd have to call the experience a plus. But it felt anything but positive in the living of it.

## Chapter Nine

**My new life wasn't all about new**, of course. It was more about going to work and going to meetings than anything else. And going to the gym. An overdose of aerobics had been my salvation during The Year of Change. While Bobby was bottoming out and recovering, I was discovering how a little extra oxygen to the brain works wonders. I was hooked. And I started to pump a little, too. On machines, mind you—no free-weight madness for me. And there I was, in my early forties, with the best body of my life. It was all good.

The employment challenge in my new life was difficult enough. But then there was the "dating game." *I can't believe I'm going to have to start dating!* I told myself. The last time I was single—in 1975—the rules were simple: fuck first and ask questions later. *And now I'm expected to go on getting-to-know-you dates? Hmmm, sounds like high school. And sober, at that. Is this really how responsible adults behave? No wonder I never wanted to be one of those.*

The first attractive men I met were Program people. But after a few tentative dates, I realized I needed to find another gene pool. *The last thing I need is to hook up with a guy who's as fucked up as I am. Friends, yes. Lovers? Run!* Work is always a good source of new blood. But I didn't have much work, at first, and then came the Famous

Department Store gig with its treachery and tension. But then there was the gym. Ah yes, body central.

The YMCA locker room was peopled entirely by men—some young, some old, some in between—whose sole purpose for attending was the quest for health and fitness. With the added amenity, for some of us, that casual contact in the steam room was always a possibility. I don't mind admitting it felt like a life saver to me. Dating? Hell no. Emotional growth? Not a bit of it. Connection? Most assuredly so. Of the carnal variety. I needed it. I was offered it. I took it. As often as possible.

I was feeling stronger—emotionally, too. And I became less fearful of all the twists and turns that are possible in life. I was beginning to spread my wings. I won't call it soaring, but there were definitely some practice flights. And I learned to trust that I had a right to a full and joyous life, no matter how many mistakes I made.

Bobby had his own, parallel process. I was pleased to learn he teamed up with a new flame. Another Southern white boy some years his junior. I knew Allen slightly. And I knew that Bobby was very fond of him. So I was not surprised to learn they had started a relationship. I was a bit relieved, I think, to see Bobby moving on. It lessened—very slightly—my considerable feelings of guilt about how the last years had played out.

I knew already that Bobby was a cheerful ex. I had met several of his exes through the years. They were good old friends. I doubted my ability to be such a good sport. Maybe in the future? Some day? Some year? But not now. Bobby got it. Of course. And he let me define the terms of our new relationship. He gave me space. He stopped calling for any reason other than some business of ours that needed my attention.

I'm guessing it was just about six months after the breakup that I happened to see Bobby on First Avenue, and we stopped for a chat. It was always a delight to see him, even when the delight was dampened by the percolation of old feelings.

"How are you?" Bobby asked.

"Well. Very well, actually. It's a stupid job, but it's just for now, not forever," I said.

"You know that red raincoat you always liked? I replaced it, and you should have it, if you still want it. I know it fits you, better than it ever did me."

"Yes, thanks, Bobby. I'm off on Tuesday, so I'll give you a call and stop by for it," I said.

"No, I'll leave it with your doorman this week. I pass the building every day."

"Thanks, Sweetie. That's very kind of you." I nearly said, *I love you.* That would have been the truth, of course. But it was impossible to say. Just then. "And how are you?" I asked.

"Doing well, thanks. I didn't want to bother you with it, but I had hernia surgery a few weeks ago. It went well, and I'm mending nicely."

"Ouch!" I said. "That runs in my family. So, I'm probably next. Don't be surprised if I call to ask the name of your surgeon."

"Take care, Sunshine," Bobby said as he kissed me good-bye and we went our separate ways. It was at that moment I knew: Whatever else happened, however our paths might cross—or not—in the years to come, it was over. I was free; I was off-duty, for sure, on the suicide watch. I would never nurse Bobby through another illness. My life was no longer his, but mine alone. And the keen sense of relief I hoped for was blunted by another keen sense—loss. And loss held the upper hand.

# Chapter Ten

**It was about 9:00 that Tuesday morning** when the phone rang. This was before caller ID, so it was always a gamble. I picked up.

"Sunny!"

"Anita, it has to be you. You're the only one who calls me Sunny. How are you?" I asked, as I experienced a big rush of Provincetown memories.

"As well as can be expected for an old lady. And you?

"Better than I have any right to be, I guess. It's such a treat to hear your voice, Anita. I can't even tell you."

"Likewise, I'm sure," she said in her best imitation of a '30s movie gangster moll.

"Now I'm getting nervous," I said, knowing that she and her husband were hardly kids.

"No, no," she said, "I'm fine, and Moises is fine—if older and fatter than he should be. Look who's talking! I'm calling to tell you I'm coming to New York next month. It's just for a few days. I joined a sort of ladies' reading circle, or whatever you want to call it. I thought I'd hate it, but I've made some friends, actually. We have outings, and this year we decided to go to New York to see some museums and galleries."

"I don't think there's anything that would make me happier right now than to see your lovely face again," I said.

"You'll have to settle for what's left of it," Anita said.

"Likewise, I'm sure," I said.

"We're arriving on the 27th. I can't remember the name of the hotel—Edison, maybe, or, well, whatever. I'll let you know. The first big outing is the next day. To the Metropolitan. I'm sure I told you about the time Moises and I brought Paul to New York."

"Yes, of course," I said. The miniature portrait of their son Paul that Anita gave me all those years before was still precious to me.

"Well, glorious as it is, I just don't think I can go back to the Met. So, I wondered if I could take you to lunch, instead.

"Yes, of course," I said. "I'll cook for you."

"No," she said. "You have enough going on in your life, I think, without having to . . . Sunny, please choose a restaurant for the two of us for lunch on the 28th.

"Done," I said.

"I'm happy to join the girls at the Whitney, and the Modern, and however many galleries in SOHO. But I just don't think I could. . ."

"Anita, I'm delighted," I said.

"Thanks, Sunny," she said. "I'll call next week with the details."

"Please give Moises my very best . . . my love, actually,"

"Of course," Anita said.

"I haven't had many big Portuguese bears in my life," I said.

"Sunny! *That* big Portuguese bear is mine! But I have to tell you, he's the one who said to me, 'If you're really going to New York, you have to call Sunny.' "

"Moises said that?"

"And he also considered joining me on the trip. For a minute. And then he said, 'I think you should go and have a wonderful time. But I can't do it.' And that was that."

"Yes," I said.

"So I'll call next week. Looking forward!" And we hung up. I meant what I said: I was delighted to hear from Anita. She had been such an important part of the Summer of '76. And other than Christmas cards, we really hadn't any contact all these years. I was happy to find a restaurant for us and to rearrange my work schedule a bit to have that day off.

📖

I arrived at the hotel nearly fifteen minutes early. I didn't want Anita to wait for me alone in the lobby. It *was* the Edison—a favorite of generations of bargain travelers to New York City. The concierge assured me the ladies had already set out on their morning adventure. I assured him that Mrs. Lopes had not. And of course she answered her room phone and then came right down.

Anita looked great. *She must be close to seventy,* I thought. *And it suits her.* "Anita, I want some of that youth serum you've been using," I said.

"If *you* get any younger, we'll have to put you back in diapers," she said.

"Don't rush me!" I said. "Anita, it's so good to see you. I didn't know when—or if—I'd see you again. And, here we are."

"Sunny, I can't tell you! I almost backed out of this trip. But I promised you lunch, and so where are we going?"

"Yes," I said. "First things first. I thought it might be fun to go to Colombetta. It's only a couple of blocks, so we can walk."

"Let's do it," Anita said. And we set out.

"The owner did an event for us at the store," I told Anita. "She was charming, and she invited me to her Valentine's Day festivities. Thank God my old tuxedo still fits. I don't think we'll have dancing today, but I think lunch will be nice anyway."

"No, no, I never dance before 5:00," Anita said.

"Good, so that's settled," I said. I wore a blazer, to smarten up a bit for the surroundings. But I hoped not to have to wear a tie on my day off. We walked up to the main floor, and the maître d' escorted us to a corner table. Nothing was said about my lack of necktie. So far, so good. The gilded surroundings looked even more so in the noontime light. And yet it felt welcoming as well.

We ordered a glass of wine and started to look at the menu. And then the owner walked over. I stood and kissed her on both cheeks, of course. "Leila, your restaurant is every bit as beautiful during the day as it is at night."

"All the better for having you in it," she said. "Welcome," and she gave Anita a lovely peach-colored rose.

"Please meet Anita Lopes, one of my oldest friends," I said.

"I think you could have phrased that better," Anita said.

"Anita, please meet Leila Meglioro, who I suspect understood what I meant," I said. The women greeted each other. And then we were on our own to make some dining decisions. "Her father started this restaurant in 1906, if you can believe it," I said. "And then decades later he married and had one child. So Leila and her mother ran the restaurant together for years. And now it's just hers. Her husband is Austrian, by the way, and he's a research scientist at Rockefeller University." He was not yet a Nobel Laureate. That came at the end of the decade. "Is that enough background?"

"Sunny, I've missed you. But not your lectures. What should I order?"

"Something veal, I think," I said. And we did order something veal. One of us had the sauté with lemon and capers, and one of us had a sauté with mushrooms and cream. I can't remember which was which. And, of course, it doesn't matter.

"We heard about you and Bobby," Anita said. "I was worried about you. But I knew you'd get it right."

"I'm glad someone has confidence in my abilities," I said. "That's more than I have, often."

"I always thought you were stronger and smarter than *you* thought you were," Anita said. Tears started to well up in my eyes. We finished our veal dishes, and then the waiter cleared our plates and brought little salads. "Moises cried after you left Provincetown."

"What?"

"Like a baby. Like he never cried after Paul died," Anita said. My heart was pulled right back into the accident on the fishing boat that Anita told me about, that spilled their son's life blood into the sea and changed their lives forever.

"How did you survive that, anyway?" I asked. "I'm about to lose my dog, and there are times when I go into crying jags and don't know quite how to get out of them. And that's for a *pet*, for Christ's sake!" It was more than that, of course. I think Anita knew. But we didn't go there.

"Losing a child is something that should never happen to anyone, not even your worst enemy. But it does," Anita said. "And then, I think—eventually—you have to decide whether you want to go on living or not. Paul was so full of life and so loving. I didn't want to let him down. That was it, really. I knew that if I didn't keep my heart strong he would be lost forever.

"I don't know what the process was for Moises. We never talked about it much. There just didn't seem to be any words. Only feelings. And they were too raw to handle. And then, in a few years, the loss grew into daily life. And it became as unremarkable as breakfast. I think that was when I decided to spend five minutes every morning, when I wake up, remembering my beautiful boy. And thanking God I had him as long as I did."

Anita and I were both feeling a bit wrung out, so I changed the subject. "How about dessert?" I asked. "They make a delicious custard here."

"Now you're speaking my language," Anita said. "Yes, the custard. And maybe they have some fresh raspberries to go with it."

"I'll ask. Anita, it's so good to see you. I've felt—unreal this year. As if the past never even happened. But talking with you—just the way we did seventeen years ago—takes me right back. I have a mother, you know. I think you'd like her. She's smart, independent, talented, WASPy—very like you in many ways, and yet worlds away in others. But this child could still use another mother. Would you consider taking me on?"

"As if I didn't have enough to worry about," Anita said. "Moises needs me more every day, and now you want me to take on another project?"

"Yes, please," I said. "It's what we boys crave. I won't ask for much."

"Yeah, sure," Anita said. "I've heard that before."

"All I ask is for you to include *me* in that morning prayer, or whatever you call it, when you remember Paul. And if you agree, I'll pledge to hold the two of you—the *three* of you—in my heart as long as I live. It's not much, but it's all I have to give just now."

"It's a deal," Anita said, and we shook hands on it.

Dessert was a welcome distraction. The custard was very good, as I predicted. And they did have raspberries to go with it, plus blackberries and blueberries. And the coffee was also good. And then it was time for me to let go. "What are you going to do with yourself this afternoon?" I asked.

"The girls won't be back until 5:00 or 6:00, I expect. So I'll write some postcards and grab a little nap before dinner. Thanks, Sunny, for looking after the old lady," Anita said.

I wouldn't have missed it," I said. "I don't know when I'll get back to P'town. I'm not really thinking about holidays right now. I have to make some sense of my career and my life."

"You *will* make sense of it all, Sunny. And when you do, you'll relax for a minute and come to visit us.

You know, you could stay in Paul's room. I hadn't thought of that, but we have plenty of space."

"Thank you so much, Anita, but I couldn't do that to you. Too much work."

"I'm sure you're no trouble at all," Anita said.

"Forget it, Lady. I'm not going to have you waiting on me. But I will come to visit. Promise."

"Good," Anita said. "So that's settled. Walk me back to the hotel?"

"Of course," I said, and we set out.

Saying good bye to Anita was difficult. Sometimes I wonder if it isn't easier to just isolate myself. Less wear and tear on the heart, maybe. No relationships, no pain. But no chance of that for me. No, I have to reach out, and then deal with the consequences. On the way home I started thinking about a fish class coming up the next month. *Something Portuguese,* I thought. *Yes, P'town Portuguese is the way to go. Might as well use every experience.*

# Chapter Eleven

**All sorts of people** walked through housewares at Famous Department Store. Half of New York and half of its tourists, too. I used to joke that on those rare occasions when I came down with a head cold, Technicolor phlegm announced that the virus came from some exotic corner of the globe. Nothing home-grown ever looked like that.

I shouldn't have been surprised—but I was—when who should walk up and greet me one after-noon but an old flame. And I hadn't seen him in twenty years! Fred Apolinario was my first real boy-friend. I fell in puppy love with Fred in Venice. How could I not? I was twenty-one. He was twenty-five, I think. Twenty-six, tops. And he was my history instructor. It was textbook stuff.

Fred's about my height, medium build, dark hair and mustache, as I remember. He had a trim beard at one point. Fred smoked a pipe and cultivated all manner of Anglo academic affectations, learned at English universities. So he was a tea snob, for in-stance, which I quite liked. He also spoke Italian and had some grounding in food and wine. He was the perfect mentor for that Venice adventure.

We met the day I arrived at the palazzo. We all assembled that first evening in the living room with the big windows onto the Grand Canal. After getting-to-know-you drinks and then dinner that evening in the dining room, I knew that Fred would be my lover. I think he knew it too. He invited me to his room, if not that same night then the next. We fell into bed. The sex was good. Not great, but it was adequate—good enough to keep me coming back for more the entire term, and beyond. And, of course, it isn't really about the sex, anyway, is it? Certainly not after the first flush.

What attracted me to Fred was his learning, and his gentle affection for me. He taught me to love E M Forster and Mary Renault. I came to feel very tenderly toward his foibles and his hurts. Such sad eyes, I always thought. Even in the sketches from that restaurant in Venice, from a festive evening, you can see it. I still have them, both—his and my portraits. What was that sadness about? I guess I didn't really know him very well.

We found ways to sneak around the palazzo—and even Venice itself, especially at night—without detection. Well, nearly so. The director's wife knew what was going on, and she was not amused. But I was twenty-one, after all, so she had no valid grounds for discipline. And I admitted nothing, of course. It was obvious to me that our relationship was none of her fucking business. So I was not about to give her grist for her mill.

Fred and I continued our relationship, as discreetly as possible. Not only did we meet in the most romantic city on the planet, but we shared weekends in Verona, in Desanzano on Lake Garda, and in Arezzo in a little *pensione* right across the street from the church of San Francesco. I saw Florence for the first time with Fred. And Bologna. And the historical sites in Ravenna.

I was smitten. After a lovely holiday trip to Strasbourg, Paris, London, and Edinburgh—all student stuff, done on the cheap, but still wonderful—we parted. He was headed back to Venice for the second term. I was headed home, after a month in Rome, actually. I can't say that all of this flashed into my consciousness that spring afternoon when Fred walked up to my demo station and extended his hand. Chunks of it, for certain. "It's good to see you!" I said, while thinking all sorts of other things.

"And you. I saw your picture in the ad, and thought I'd say hello," he said. So, our meeting was not accidental. The department store had just run a big ad with a tiny picture of me announcing I was their new "culinary specialist." So, Fred saw it and decided to drop by.

There was an awkward silence that I decided to fill. "Goodness, it must be twenty years!" I said, and decided to go academic. "I've been doing all sorts of things. I wrote a food book that came out in 1984."

"Yes, I know. I read the review in *The New York Times* and bought a copy."

How surprised was I? I didn't mention that the book was printed in Verona. It was too bizarre. "And I wrote another one, a fish cookery book, that came out in 1989."

"Yes, I know. That got some good mentions in *The Times*, too."

I couldn't believe that my old flame had been keeping up with me! From a deep distance. He suggested dinner, and I was happy to accept. We had history. We settled on a date and time. I asked for his phone number so that I could delay decisions, for a bit, on the venue. I wanted to get it right. Fred supplied his number. He left, and I pretended to go back to work. Mostly, I jumped upon the decision at hand.

An Italian restaurant would have been a bit obvious. And probably not authentic enough. Instead I chose a dark little Middle Eastern restaurant on St. Mark's Place. I knew the food would be good. And I couldn't resist the irony of our dining in New York's San Marco rather than in Venice's. Was I all aflutter on my way to dinner? No, not really. But I had done my share of "Will he like me?" during the day: the nonsense we put ourselves through even when the stakes are maybe not so high.

Fred was waiting for me when I arrived. "You look great," he said.

"So do you," I said. He did look remarkably unchanged by the years.

"What a fun place this is. I had no idea it was here," he said.

"I think you'll like the food." I said.

"I'm sure I will." So far so good.

We ordered wine and appetizers: little dumpling things with lamb in a spicy broth, and crispy dumplings with vegetables and sesame. We could have waited a bit for the rest of our dinner order, but I suggested we move on. We decided on a grilled chicken dish with a rice *palaw*, and a meat stew with spinach and fresh fenugreek leaves. I began to relax. I'm always a bit tense until the food choices are out of the way. Even when I've ordered the wrong thing, at least the decisions have been made and I'm forced to let go and allow them to play out. Is ordering dinner a lot like life? Maybe so.

"Did you really go to law school?" I asked. That was his intention when we last met in New York. It seemed odd, because Fred already had two degrees in history from English universities. But hey, people do make choices.

"Yes," he said. "I went back to Fordham and finished up as quickly as possible. I practice corporate law. We specialize in international relations. Most of it is exceptionally boring, but I get to travel a lot. So that's good. I like it, actually. More than teaching."

"Did you ever think I would be a teacher?" I asked.

"Maybe sex education," Fred said.

"I thought about that, but all the good jobs were taken," I said. "So I decided on cooking instead."

"What do you teach, actually?" Fred asked.

"Oh, all sorts of things. Basic skills, often, or Into to Just About Any Cuisine You Can Imagine. Even a little Italian here and there. You may not think I was a very good student—no comments, please—but I soaked up a lot. Only recently I realized that I have a frame of reference for Italian dishes and flavors and techniques. And it's all because of Venice. And you. 'Yes, that tastes Italian,' or, 'No, that's not right.' I have a colleague who's a protégé of Stefano Aureglio, the great Tuscan master, so I've learned a lot from her that I missed back then. But everything she makes looks and tastes just right. Because it's Italian. And I get it, I hope. Well, anyway, I like teaching," I said. "It keeps me on my toes. One step ahead of the students."

"Tell me," Fred said. "I learned more than even I wanted to know about Venice, so that I could teach your little group. You were an interesting bunch."

"Yes," I said. "The two guys who palled around—the chunky one with the handlebar mustache you called Ungar, and the skinny one with the big nose—

they were maybe the only ones who weren't screwing someone else in the group, or the extended family."

"No, we weren't the only ones who shattered the Commandments, were we?" Fred asked.

"It was fun, wasn't it?" I said.

"Yes. Great fun. How does it feel to be teacher's pet?"

"I loved it," I answered. "I would have kept the job if you had wanted me."

"It was never a question of wanting you. I never stopped that. I just didn't think you were making sense about employment and paying the rent and assuming responsibilities. Adult stuff."

"Yes, adult stuff," I said. "I'm coming late to that. But I'm loyal, you can give me that. Well, almost." Did he just tell me that he never stopped wanting me? Yes, that's what my old flame told me. And that he let our relationship die because of my immaturity. And I countered with a claim of a constant heart. I, who had just abandoned Bobby. Hmm . . .

The food was really good. We ate everything and ordered a salad and some more wine. "I have a new job in Princeton," Fred said. "It starts in two months. I can't face a commute like that, so I'm going to move." To be perfectly honest, I don't remember whether the new job was at the university or in the town of Princeton. But I suddenly realized that Fred was husband hunting! He didn't want to move to New Jersey alone. That was it, really. And he thought perhaps I might be the one. I was flattered, of course. It's always nice to be thought of as husband material. But it also felt a bit mechanical. Hmm. Need mate. Find mate. No longer alone.

Dining with Fred, two decades after our affair ended, I realized that I had gotten over him ages before. The thrill was long gone. Our meetings in New York—on my annual visits in the years after Venice—had grown increasingly unpleasant, until I stopped reaching out to him. And that was fine. By the time I moved to New York with Bobby at the end of 1975, I wasn't thinking of Fred at all. And once I had enjoyed the brief flutter of lost romance that spring evening in 1993, the last thing I wanted was to backtrack.

After very good coffee and little sweets that were achingly so, it was time to leave. We strolled slowly toward the subway and enjoyed the muted bustle of a spring evening when everyone is eating and drinking and celebrating the fact that they are alive and not alone. Before descending to our separate trains, we said our good nights and shared a kiss. St. Mark's Place is nothing like Venice. Worlds away. But we had spent a pleasant evening with really good food and really good conversation. It was enough. I wondered if I would ever see Fred again. Probably not, I guessed. And I was okay with that.

Fred found his new mate! It wasn't me, of course, but there was a guy who worked in another department at Famous Department Store who caught his eye. Maybe even the same day Fred came to see me. Cute, young guy. Animated. Silly. It seemed to me he was a bit of a lightweight in the intelligence department. So I wondered what sort of partner he would make for Mr. Giant Brain. But they started dating. And a month later the kid quit his job and they moved to Princeton together. I have no idea where that all went, but I wished them both every happiness and still do.

## Chapter Twelve

**When Heidi called to tell me** that she and Liz were bringing their son to New York for a few days, I was quite moved by all the Provincetown memories that came flooding back. We hadn't spoken since Bobby and I left the Cape that summer, 1976. I heard somehow that Liz's pregnancy went well, and that she had a boy. But the fact of that event was off somewhere in my fog zone until Heidi's call jolted it into reality. The child was how old now, fifteen! How could that be possible?

The boy's father, Heath, was my prime memory. Ah, yes. Heath Woodford occupied a big ol' chunk of my fantasyland that summer. Heath was, well, for me, part Robin Hood and part wet dream. And when he was killed in a senseless car crash that summer, just two months after he supplied the seed for his best friend's new family, I grieved big time. As much as I knew how to grieve. In those days.

Heidi had the same solid, capable qualities that Heath had. I always thought her more like his little brother than his best friend from their childhoods in Halifax. She was both, really. And Liz was so very different, so bubbly, so joyous. When the two of them told me about the pregnancy, I was pleased for them, of course. But it took a while to process it, because I was really mostly thinking about Heath. And myself.

After Heidi's phone call, I started to think about the boy, and I realized how perfectly the choices were made. For Heidi and Liz to have a child with Heath's sperm was as close to their having a child together as humans can manage, at this point in the history of genetics. And I felt awash in joy for them and their accomplishment.

We met at the Metropolitan Museum of Art, the first stop on any proper cultural tour of New York. I didn't even question how the Met could be figuring in my life again, so soon after Anita's visit. It felt natural. The south wing of the main floor—where the Greek and Roman department is now—still had that nice restaurant with the big fountain oval in the center. Those who visited in those years will also remember the little espresso bar just inside, in the northwest corner of the room, that was backed by a charming big smoke and gold mirror/mural salvaged from the great liner SS Normandy before it was scrapped. Anyone uncertain of the Art Deco style would do well to stare at that mirror for a bit. The answers are all there.

I still miss that little bar and the big restaurant, but, hey, time marches on. The statuary looks great in that space now. I wouldn't have evicted the eateries, but like so many other situations in life, it's none of my business. The girls looked great. Older, of course, but exactly as I remembered them. Heidi was just as tall and serious as before, and Liz was just as easy and energetic as before. I greeted them with genuine affection, and they returned it. And then there was the son. Fifteen years old! How was that possible?

The girls named him Cliff. He was nearly as tall as his dad, about six feet. His coloring was a bit darker, more like Liz's. Not so gingery as Heath's. I think it's the freshness that draws us to young people. But Cliff also had an easy grace about him that made him so stunning that I was quite shaken. Because he was handsome? Because he was sexy? Because he was so full of promise? Or was it because he had Heath's eyes?

"What color would you say Heath's eyes were? I always thought golden brown," I said.

"Some people called it hazel," Heidi said. "That sounded odd to me. I called it caramel."

"Well, I can tell you, Cliff," I said. "One late afternoon that summer we were having a drink on the little porch in the back of the Pilgrim House. When the sunlight came in from horizon level it set your dad's eyes on fire, whatever color they were. He was one of the most beautiful men God ever created. Even the sunlight worshiped him. I was a little bit in love with him, that summer before you were born. But then, so was everyone else."

I was gobsmacked by a flood of memories—the impending arrival of Hurricane Belle, a deer darting in front of Heath's pickup, a crash, a somber trip to the hospital in Hyannis, the overnight vigil while the storm raged over us, and the horrible reality of Heath's death early that morning. I didn't even know that I hadn't finished with it. I could have told you that I had moved on. I could have sworn that I had gotten through my mourning. Done and finished. Fat chance.

Lunching in that café was all about the setting. But the food was perfectly adequate, if not memorable. We ordered some salady things and fizzy water. I asked the waiter if he could put a splash of grenadine in Cliff's glass. "Of course," he said, and returned with a whole pitcher of mocktails. Cliff was getting so much attention from the handsome young waiter that he blushed very slightly. But mostly Cliff smiled and accepted the attention politely. *He's been there before,* I thought, *and he'd better get used to it.*

"Your uncle," I started to say to Cliff, and then I couldn't remember Heath's partner's name.

"Richard," Heidi reminded me.

"Of course," I said. "I haven't seen him since the memorial. What a sweet man. How is he?"

"Uncle Richard is doing great," Cliff told me. "He still lives in Halifax. I get up to see him at least twice a year. Him and Grandma. Sometimes for a month or so. He taught me to sail. And next year we're planning a trip to Bermuda." There was a noticeable reaction from Heidi and Liz. "Well, we'll see. The moms are not so keen on that."

"No, they are not," Liz answered for them both.

"I'd stay ashore if I were you," I said. "Richard won't remember me, but please tell him that I fell in love with him that memorial afternoon on MacMillan Pier. Those baby blue eyes of his were pools of despair, and I would have done anything to comfort him. But there was nothing I could do, of course, so I just gave him my heart. Tell him he can string mine on his belt with all the others. We can never have too many, after all. I don't suppose he gets down to Provincetown too often."

"No," Cliff said. " 'Too many memories,' he says."

"Yes," I said. "I haven't been there, well, not since Bobby and I left that summer." The food arrived, and we all welcomed the distraction, I think. We were quiet for a bit as we munched and remembered.

And then Heidi said, "I was thinking of Bunny this morning. He always said, 'Get that boy to the Met, and it doesn't matter whether it's pictures or singing. Just get him there.' And here we are."

"I think *Tosca* will wait for your next visit," I said. "This is a perfect start." Ah, Bunny Babbitt. What an exquisitely outrageous—and talented—man. I had carried him with me all those years, even when I didn't quite know why. And suddenly it was 1976 again. It all came back to me: Jan Carter's drag impressions and his showroom, the Madeira Room, in the Pilgrim House hotel. And of course, the early show with her highness, Bunny Babbitt, the funniest, most pansexual performer I've ever known.

I knew Bunny loved me. Randy told me so— Randy Ball, Jan's dancer that summer. I saw Randy last in 1986, just as he was leaving New York to go south to die. And Randy gave me a photo of Bunny and me that was on Bunny's night table when he died. And that was just about me. I knew Bunny would be a fierce protector of Heath's child.

"Bunny was the best babysitter," Liz said. "Not only did he look after Cliff, but he also did the dishes."

"Bunny used to tell me I'm a wizard," Cliff said. "For my sixth birthday he gave me a wand and told me I can use it to create anything I desire. I believed him. I still do. But then when he died the next year, all I really wanted was to have him back."

"Even the most powerful wizards get tripped up by that one," I said.

"Yes. And yet . . ."

"You sometimes feel him breathing down your neck."

"How did you know?" Cliff exclaimed.

"Because he's stayed with me, all these years. And he loved you much more than he ever loved me, I'm certain. So, Bunny will never leave you. Don't be afraid to talk to him. He's always listening. And he gives pretty good advice, as I'm sure you know."

"Yes," Cliff said. "Good advice."

The waiter cleared away the lunch things and asked Cliff, "Is there something else you desire?" Cliff blushed in earnest that time. But it was all so wholesome that even the moms chuckled a bit.

"Ice cream, please. Chocolate," Cliff said.

"And may I suggest a shortbread with that?"

"Yes, thank you," Cliff said. The moms ordered tea, and I ordered a coffee.

"So, what's on tap for your visit?" I asked.

"All the usual touristy stuff," Liz said. "The Empire State Building, the Statue of Liberty, like that."

"Perfect, I said. You have to do that. At least once. I'd be tempted to go with you, except that I'm working. Don't forget to go to Rockefeller Center. I still think it's wonderful. It's spring, so there won't be any ice skating or Christmas trees, but I'll bet there's a flower show, or something nice. And the architecture of the whole complex is so stunning. I can never remember which building it is, but be sure to ask the guards which murals are the ones that cover the Diego Rivera works that Nelson Rockefeller ordered destroyed. All history is important, even the ugly parts."

"What about the World Trade Center?" Heidi asked. "Do you think we should go there?"

"I don't know what to tell you," I said. "I had dinner once in the restaurant at the top of whichever tower it is. Once was enough for me. And I visited a friend who worked in a big investment company, on a very windy afternoon when the tower was swaying noticeably. Again, once was enough for me. Why don't you save that for the next trip? In case you get bored with life at street level." I didn't want to nix it, but I also thought they could find a better use for their time.

"We have tickets for something at the Music Hall tonight," Liz said.

"Perfect!" I said. "I was about six when my parents took me there, and the memory is indelible. And Broadway is not going to disappear. So you'll go to a play next trip."

The waiter returned with beverages—which were unremarkable—and a big ice cream sundae extravaganza for Cliff. There were no sparklers, but just about anything else you can imagine.

"And it's not even my birthday," Cliff said.

"But it's your first visit to the Met," the waiter said, "so it's the same thing."

"Exactly!" I said. I sipped my coffee and retreated into my observer shell for a bit. They were clearly having a good time, this little family: these two old friends from what seemed a distant past, and their wonderful young creation. I felt like an intruder on the intimacy of their lives, and yet, they had invited me in.

Cliff finished the sundae, of course. We all know that teens can down heroic quantities of food without ill effects. But I sensed—and I would stake my life on it—that Cliff would have preferred a few polite bites. Except that he had just been gifted—for no

87

good reasons other than that he was young, beautiful, and very much alive—by a nice man who was concerned only with Cliff's happiness. And so Cliff packed away the entire ice cream creation. And then thanked the waiter again. It was at that moment— precisely when he thanked the cute waiter again— that I realized I had fallen permanently in love with him.

After our luncheon, the little family was headed for the Old Masters, of course. It would have been fun to watch a handsome youngster encountering glorious paintings for the first time. So many of them are so precious in the depths of my memories. Transformational, even. I could have lectured about Whistler and Velazquez, and Titian. But I reminded myself that if Cliff wanted a lecture, he could always call me. And perhaps he would.

Art history? Yes, I was available. How to choose a good suit? Yes, available. How to dress for seduction? Yes, available. Choosing the right colors for one's coloring? Yes, available. Whole or clarified butter in a *sauce hollandaise*? Yes, available. High heat or low heat when roasting a chicken? Yes, available. Fucking on the first date? Yes, available. The best way to ask for a date? Yes, available. The virtues of a nice rosé in warm weather? Yes, available. The right underwear for a young man? Yes, available. The most romantic restaurant in New York? Yes, available. The most romantic dish to cook for a new flame? Yes, available. The way to ensure it will be forever? Not so much.

In the end, I left the three of them to fend for themselves, secure in the knowledge that whichever way they ventured in their tour of the Metropolitan they would find exquisite beauty. And I knew that in three or four hours they would experience beauty burnout. I only hoped that Cliff would feel the need to return. Often. For those who fall under her spell, the Met is a lifetime obsession. Would Cliff become one of her lovers? I hoped yes. But I also knew that it was beyond my feeble powers to influence him one way or another, any more than I could convince him to be gay or straight.

As we were saying our good-byes, I said to him, "You're going to be a real heartbreaker, Cliff. Let them down easy!" I knew Heidi and Liz had taught him respect for women. That would take him far. I felt confident that he was a good boy and that he would soon be a good man, like his father. When I hugged him, he hugged me back, and gave me a surprise peck on the cheek. I hated the parting. I won't go so far as to say it was like losing Heath all over again, but it did leave an unexpected void in my heart.

"You have my phone number. If there's anything you ever need, please call me," I said. Cliff promised he would, and then the three of them decided that I should be an honorary uncle. "Does that make me blood kin?" I asked.

"It makes you whatever you want to be," Heidi said.

"Then I want it all," I said. "Cliff, don't forget: I'm family now. You can't just ignore me in future."

"How could I ignore my New York uncle?" Cliff asked.

"Quite easily," I said. "But don't!"

"I'll never ignore you, Unc," Cliff said.

"I have witnesses," I said, referring to the mothers and our new waiter friend.

"I swear!" Cliff said, raising his right hand.

"Don't," I said. "Just promise to have a wonderful life and to love as many people as you can. That's all the attention I need."

"Yes, Sir!"

"And don't call me sir!"

"Yessir," Cliff said. And then I stopped dangling him and said truly final good-byes. They headed into the galleries, and I headed home. I felt somehow that a nap would do me more good than another few hours at the Met. And of course, there was recipe work waiting for me at my desk. After my nap, I promised myself.

## Chapter Thirteen

**When the phone rang** the following evening, I left it for the answering machine. "Hi, it's Cliff," came over the speaker. I dashed to the phone and nearly tripped over poor old Scooter on my way.

"Hi, Cliff," I said, casually. "It's good to hear from you."

"The moms wanted me to call and thank you for joining us for lunch."

"That's because they were brought up properly," I said.

"But, actually, I'm the one who wanted to call."

"Oh?"

"I want to hear more about my father. They don't really want to talk about him, and Uncle Richard . . .well, he just can't. Bunny used to talk about him as if he were still alive. And now Bunny's gone. And there's no one else. So, I have Dad's eyes, and his chin. But what does all that mean? You seem to know something."

"Cliff, I'd open a vein if I could bring Heath back," I said. "As would Richard. As would Heidi. As would Liz. As would your grandmother. But it doesn't work that way. Things happen. And all the people who love you are just trying to get on with it the best they can. And speaking of people who love you, may I be permitted to join the ranks?"

"Yes."

"Thank you for that gift," I said. "When do you leave?"

"Day after tomorrow."

"Well, I don't know. Find me an hour, tomorrow morning, maybe. I have an evening class but not all that much going on until I have to shop for it. Why don't you come by the apartment? I'll make an omelet. Please don't tell me you're allergic to eggs."

"I love eggs," said Cliff.

"Good. Tell Heidi and Liz exactly what you're up to. They deserve complete honesty."

"Yes."

"Well, then, 10:00 tomorrow?"

"Thank you."

"Well, we'll see," I said. "Thank me if you learn something."

Cliff showed up promptly at 10:00 the next morning. I greeted him with a hug and a very chaste kiss, and sat him down at the dining table. I had already started coffee and toasted a few slices of *brioche*. "The moms know exactly where you are and why?" I asked.

"Yes," Cliff said. Scooter took an interest, but only a slight one.

"And?" I asked as I served Cliff a coffee that was mostly hot milk.

"Good coffee," he said.

"Don't change the subject. What do you think I know that your family doesn't?"

"It's just that nobody seems to understand how I feel."

"Don't expect that to change anytime soon," I said. "Especially if you don't verbalize it. Come into the kitchen and I'll show you how to make an omelet." Cliff hung his jacket on the back of his chair and followed me into the kitchen, obediently. It's a Manhattan apartment kitchen, mind you, so a young gazelle like him has to negotiate the physical boundaries. Not so different from working in an average restaurant kitchen, actually. I like the proximity. He didn't seem to mind. We rolled up our sleeves.

"Break three eggs into that bowl, and don't crack them on the edge—too many bits of shell. Crack them here, on the board. A big pinch of salt—some people say no salt until later. I say that's bullshit, but you decide for yourself. Grind some pepper. I like lots. That's purely a matter of taste. A tablespoon of water? I'm in the yes camp. After you've made a few hundred omelets you can decide for yourself. No milk. Ever. That is not negotiable. Fork the eggs briskly until they feel combined but not destroyed. You'll learn."

*Hmm, this is a challenge*, I thought. *I'm so close to this baby I can smell his hair, not quite dry from his morning shower. He's like a foal, still damp from the womb.*

"Now let's heat the pan. Don't get me started on French steel and seasoning pans. You could spend a lifetime on that, and life's too short. Just get a good nonstick pan that's no more than nine inches across the lip, and use it just for omelets."

*He's actually paying attention*, I thought. *And he's so—endearing, that's it. Even more delightful up close than I remembered from lunch.*

93

"Medium heat—or sort of medium-high, depending upon your heat source. Let the pan get hot, but don't burn it up. If you start with a cold pan, your omelet will stick, guaranteed. Throw in a tablespoon of unsalted butter. It must sizzle. Swirl the butter all around until it melts and coats the pan. At the very instant the sizzle stops and the milk solids start to brown, pour in the eggs all at once.

*Beautiful hands*, I thought. *So like Heath's. He could be a carpenter, or a sculptor, or a surgeon, or whatever the fuck he wants to be, for that matter.*

"Pause for two seconds only. You're right-handed? Grab the pan with your left hand and start to pull the pan quickly fore and aft, while at the same time, you hold the fork in your right hand with the tines flat, almost against the pan—but don't scrape it!—and move the fork clockwise to keep the eggs in motion. When they start to set but are still very moist, lift the handle so the eggs start to head for the far end of the pan.

*He's so young!*, I thought. *And yet so substantial. That's it, really. He's a fully formed person. At fifteen!*

"Use the fork to coax the near edge of the eggs to roll down the pan. Rap the pan on the stove smartly two or three times, to settle the mass at the far end. Quickly put down the fork and switch hands, using an underhand grip on the pan this time. Now grab a plate with your left hand and bring the plate and the pan together. Coax the far edge of the omelet out onto the plate, then let the rest of it fall onto itself, forming a perfect oval. Once the eggs go in, the whole thing takes no more than 30 seconds."

The first omelet turned out reasonably well, and then we made another. It was slightly better. We glazed them lightly with a chunk of butter speared on the tip of a knife, and then we headed for the table. I wanted Cliff to have the better one, and he seemed properly amazed that anything so simple can be so delicious. *He's a good student,* I thought. But what I said was, "Cliff, what do you want to know?"

"I've seen pictures. I've heard so many stories. But I don't really think I know him. Who was my father?"

Yeah, like I had answers to Cliff's deepest questions. Or my own, for that matter. "I'm sure everyone has told you how handsome he was. Even more so in person than in pictures. But it's way more than that. He was so solid. So reliable. I would have gone to bed with him in a millisecond, given the chance. But I was never given that chance. Because he and Richard had a bond. Instead, Heath gave me his friendship. And that was a gift.

"This is a little 'out there' and you may not want to hear it, Cliff, but I would have been proud to bear Heath's child myself. And I don't think I've ever had a fantasy like that about another man. When I heard that Liz had conceived you, I thought, *Fuck, yes! The precious seed is sown! On to the harvest!* And you, my child, are the exquisite fruit. If you'll pardon the expression."

"I've been called worse," Cliff said.

"Heath completed Richard's life, as you know, and he naturally wanted to help his best friend complete *her* family. I'm sure the moms have told you how much he was looking forward to your arrival. He saved my life once, did they tell you that?

"One Fourth of July? Was that you?" Cliff asked.

"Yes, and I'll bet it was just around the time you were conceived. I would never have survived that

95

Race Point rip current if Heath hadn't come splashing out to me and wrapped his arm around me. Terrified as I was, I knew it would be okay. Because it was Heath. And he was so *capable.* So nothing bad could happen to me. And nothing did.

"There's only one other thing I can tell you that maybe no one else knows. I showered with him once. Because of plumbing issues in the building. And I've never quite recovered from that experience. 'Men are not a new sensation,' as Lorenz Hart wrote—look it up—but standing naked next to your dad in that little group shower, I was overcome by the possibility of perfection in manhood. That was it, I think. Heath was so strong and yet so gentle. Modest to a fault. And always sweet-natured, even in a silly circumstance like the one we found ourselves in that afternoon: Heath needed a shower, and his only option was to take one with me. And so he did. Without any fuss. Just a slight blush.

"And yet, I have to tell you that I never felt I really knew him. So, maybe that puts us in the same boat. Except, here's the difference: Just because that fucking deer and that fucking pickup truck killed him, that doesn't mean *you*'ve lost him. Heath is coursing through your veins, every moment of every day. You have him inside you, always. He's yours, as long as you live. And maybe he'll live on in your child. I hope so."

"Could I have a hug?" Cliff asked.

"Of course," I said. I rose and embraced him. He's taller than I am, and broader than I am. And yet he seemed so fragile. I held him. Gently. As tenderly as I dared. As if he were a child. As indeed he was. As if he were *my* child. Which he was not. I drank in his sweet scent. I remembered his father and wanted to *be* Heath and to *possess* Heath, both at the same time.

Did I feel a stirring in the genital region? Of course! Did Cliff stir as well? Of course! Fifteen-year-old boys have erections about half the time. I had no idea what support Cliff needed from me. I held him. I waited. He clung to me. I wanted to be as solid as the Rock of Gibraltar for him. He cried a little, not wanting me to see his tears. Eventually, I took his exquisite young face in my hands and kissed him very lightly. And he said to me, "If I ever . . . made love . . . with a guy, I'd want it to be you."

That was a serious change of landscape, of course. I gently disentangled us, got him seated, and then poured us a little more coffee. "That's very sweet, Cliff," I said. "I'm glad you think you might want me to . . . be the one. But that concept is a little too adult for today's lesson. Check back with me in three years, and if you still feel the same, it would be my greatest honor to accept." I ached. Deep down. Deep down.

"Meanwhile," I said, "you're fifteen, and you have so much to learn. I know. I was in a big ol' hurry, too. But if I had it to do over again, I'd take my time and cherish each little moment along the way. You won't, of course. But think about it, anyway. Each moment is so precious. Don't rush!

"But speaking of rushing, out of here, Young Man! I have work to do."

"Yes, Sir!"

"And don't call me sir," I said.

"Yessir."

"Cliff," I said, holding him at arms' length and gazing deeply into his beautiful eyes—Heath's eyes? No, they had become Cliff's own. "You have wonderful adventures ahead of you, and never forget that all the people who love you—and that includes me—want you to have a fabulous time of it. But don't forget to study, too. That's just as important. Education is the second brightest jewel in life, after love. Maybe. Or is it the other way around? That's for you to decide."

"Thank you," Cliff said.

"Give the moms my love," I said.

"Will do."

"Off you go," I said, turning him around and sending him out the door with a swift pat on the butt.

"Three years?" he asked.

"At least."

"Not two-and-a-half?"

"Not without a birth certificate," I said.

"I meant what I said," he tossed back at me over his shoulder.

"I never doubted your honesty for a moment," I said. "You're your father's son. Be safe!"

I watched him disappear as he turned from the hallway into the lobby. Would I ever see that beautiful sapling again? Who could say? I took off my uncle cap and settled back into real life. I allowed myself a few sobs as I cleaned up the omelet things. And I stopped to pet Scooter, who was less present than he had been in earlier years, but still my best friend. Some days it seems that loss is constant, doesn't it?

## Chapter Fourteen

**I swear Scooter taught me** the choreography for our nightly ritual: When we reached the top of our hallway, safely away from the lobby, I would release him from his leash. He would freeze, like a pointer, awaiting information. The first few times we tried it, I would hold perfectly still until neither of us could stand the suspense any longer. When I made the sudden dash for the door, he would be off like a shot, and there, long before me. And then, gradually, we refined the game. I would take two sudden steps, and freeze. And Scooter would dash not to the door but around me, and wait. Two more steps, and he would dash around again. Until we had a full routine for the length of the hall.

Our neighbor, Melanie, was also a late-night dog walker, and she loved to watch. Scooter seemed to enjoy having an audience for his performance. Maybe he did a clockwise loop and then a counterclockwise loop, etc., all the way down the hall. I could be wrong. Maybe all the loops were counterclockwise. But I enjoyed our nightly game, maybe even more than Scooter did.

He had been a family member for more than a decade. He came to us at a time when we were buoyant and hopeful. He stayed for the darker years. When he was twelve—according to the vet—he was still bouncing around like a pup. But that next year

99

he began to slow down a bit. And before long his progress was positively Shakespearean, as he gradually became sans hair, sans eyes, sans ears. He kept his teeth pretty well. But the rest of him was going.

I would have continued to feed him, walk him, and pet him without too much thought for the future had it not been for ihe Garden Moment. One morning I let Scooter out as usual, but a few minutes later he started to bark. And when I ran to the garden door to investigate, I discovered that my best friend had become disoriented, with so little input from his eyes and ears. So he just stood there in the middle of the garden and howled in fear.

I got him inside as quickly as possible and vowed to take charge. If his life had become torture for him, then I clearly had to set him free. I couldn't do it just then. No, not that day. No. Scooter may have been ready, but I was certainly not. My roommate Marcia, the New Ager, suggested that I give us a week. It seemed reasonable. I phoned the vet and made an appointment for a week hence.

And then came the death vigil. Marcia had all sorts of woo-woo advice. "Have you talked to him about it?" she asked. "He understands everything you say to him, so talk to him, and tell him what's happening and why." I hated it, but I wanted to get it right. Scooter and I had our last bath together, and after the blow-drying—the only part of grooming Scooter ever enjoyed—I sat on the toilet and held him in my arms. I rocked him, and talked to him, and prepared him for the coming event. I also tried to prepare myself, of course. I told Scooter how much I loved him. I thanked him for our time together. And I sobbed. And rocked. And he nestled in my arms without a single squirm until I was sobbed out. For then.

I carried Scooter to the vet that last time. And I was careful to wear my largest and darkest sunglasses, even though it was a gray day. It was only a few blocks. Everyone in the office was sympathetic. The woman at the desk gently requested payment in advance of the procedure. A wise policy, I'm sure. Bereaved pet owners are probably not the easiest clients to collect money from. Scooter was quiet. I held him on my lap for those last few minutes. I hugged him, and snuggled in close. I didn't really talk to him. That seemed too creepy for the waiting room. And, after all, everything had been said. And then we were ushered in.

Scooter always hated his vet, ever since the neutering. Sensible, I thought. Scooter became animated, as he had always been on the doctor's table. It took several of us to hold him down for the injection. It was horrible not only to witness but to be party to. That proud little beast did not go down easily. He fought for life right up to the last moment, which was a great exhale. More like a scream, really. And then it was over.

I stumbled home, only slightly shielded by my big shades. If anyone on the street had taken the slightest interest in me, they would have seen a weeping idiot barely navigating the sidewalk. I saw a neighbor, across the street, of course. Try going anywhere in New York City without running into someone you know. I waved and kept moving.

I made it home, let myself in, took off my sunglasses, and put the kettle on for tea. Marcia was out, mercifully, so I had the apartment to myself. Within a short while I was sitting at the dining room table with a mug of strong Darjeeling in my hands. I bent my new alcohol rules—a glass of wine with dinner, on the weekend, mostly—and added a generous slug of brandy to my tea. I toasted Scooter. And then I toasted Bobby. And then I let go for the first time, really. I thought I had been grieving, but I was about to learn what grief really is.

## Chapter Fifteen

  **It was early June,** I think, when John Alegria called from Boston to tell me that he was coming to New York for a visit, in a few weeks. I hadn't seen him since our luncheon in Boston in September of 1986. I was delighted to hear from him, of course. He was part of several of my sweetest memories from earlier, sillier, lighter, younger times. Was I still a bit in love with him? After all those years? I think I'd be a fool not to be.

John was, unquestionably, the most lovable man I ever met. He's handsome, no question. He's sexy, no question. He's emotionally available, no question. And he's guileless. Who could ask for more? All these years later I still blush a little when I think of him. But that afternoon in June when he phoned, I was mostly thinking of how I could tell him about my new life.

"Bobby and I separated in September," I announced.

"I heard," John said. "I'm sure it was very difficult for both of you."

"Yes," I said. "I'm still reeling from it, actually. But it felt like the only thing to do."

"I always thought you knew your mind and your heart," John said. I wasn't so sure about that. "I can't see you making that decision without being certain."

"Yes," I said. "I was certain. But that didn't make it much easier." It was like experiencing the feelings all over again.

"Let's talk about it when I'm in New York," John said. "Will you save some time for me that week? Lunch, or dinner, or maybe both?"

"Of course," I said. "Send me your itinerary, and I'll plug myself into it. I'll cook for you, if you like. And there's a new play I want you to see. I've seen it, but I can get you tickets. And Bobby and Mary have a new show opening soon. You're on your own there. I just can't do it right now."

"Of course," John said. "I'll be traveling with a friend I want you to meet. We're staying at a funky little hotel downtown that's just one step up from the YMCA. But you know how expensive everything is."

"Don't I!"

"I'm so glad we can get together. It's been too long," John said.

"Yes. Too long." And it was time to hang up. John Alegria! In New York! It was a delightful surprise. Did I begin to invent all sorts of romantic scenarios? Of course not. Well, maybe just a few. You know enough of my nature by now—and my clay feet—to know that I went off on all sorts of romantic tangents that had nothing to do with reality. And I felt almost giddy for the first time in years.

John and his friend arrived on a Wednesday morning. I got them matinee seats for *Bring It On*, which was a hot ticket. But I knew somebody who could manage these things. After their train arrived, they would have time to drop their bags at their hotel and then head for the theater. The tickets would be waiting for them at the box office, and then *I* would be waiting for them in front of the theater after the curtain. I had been spending all my free time on recipes for a new book, so an evening off sounded delightful—and what could be better than dinner with John Alegria?

I felt a little surge of joy as I spotted John in the crowd. He looked terrific, as always. And his red shirt accentuated his Portuguese good looks. *How does he manage to seem so at home wherever he is?* I wondered. I waved to him, and he flashed that dazzling grin of his.

I gave him a warm hug and said, "John, you're a gift for these tired eyes of mine."

"It's wonderful to see you, Old Friend," he said, "and thanks so much for getting us the tickets."

"My pleasure."

"Loved the show!" John said.

"Good. So did I," I said.

"I want you to meet Brian Matthews. I've been telling him all about you," John said.

"Ouch! And he still agreed to meet me? Brave man! Hi, Brian. Welcome to New York," I said.

"Thank you. And it's great to finally meet you," he said.

"And you're not too disappointed?" I asked.

"No, not at all," Brian said. "I was expecting a real troll, but you look perfectly pleasant."

"Looks can be deceiving," I said. "I know it's a little early for dinner, but I'll bet you two are starving," I said.

"You guessed it," John said.

"Let's walk over to Jim Adam. Have you been there?" I asked Brian.

"No, but I went to the one in London last year," he said.

"So you know it has a fun, showbiz vibe. And we can have some snacks and a glass of wine and a good visit before we get serious about dinner."

"Perfect," John said.

We got a table in a corner that was not too noisy and settled in. "Brian also works in conservation," John told me. "He was at Woods Hole for a long time, and then he was transferred to Boston last year. That's how we met."

*That's how they met?* I thought. *As in, "We met and fell in love and now we're a couple"? Shit! Where was I when John told me he was bringing someone he wanted me to meet? Am I really so self-involved that I imagined John would always love only me?* I tried to process my shock as quickly and casually as possible. "That's great!" I said. "Do I hear wedding bells?"

"Actually, we're planning a commitment ceremony in September, in Provincetown. Will you come?" John asked.

"Only if I can give you away," I said.

"I'd be deeply honored if you'd stand up for me," he said.

"I always cry at weddings," I said, "but not usually in advance of them." I dabbed at my eyes theatrically. I was crying, actually. But only a little. We were drinking and snacking at Jim Adam, after all. How emotional can a person get in that setting? Pretty emotional, I learned. I began to really look at Brian, between bites and laughs and sips and witty rejoinders, of course. Before the news he had been just some guy who was traveling with John. And now he was suddenly a life partner.

I wasn't certain whether I wanted to like Brian or not. But I did, as it turned out. Deeply. Brian is about our age and handsome in a quiet, WASPy way. Sexy, too. Not a stud muffin, but rather a teammate for the long haul. He obviously adored John. But who doesn't? And John obviously adored him. Which could have been a sticking point for me, except that I willed myself to wish John all the happiness he deserved. Which was considerable. If I had to choose a mate for John, some man who was not me? The *not me* part was a little tricky. But once I navigated beyond that, yes, Brian was obviously the one.

When Brian left the table to go to the men's, I said, "John, I like him *so much*!"

"I hoped you would. He was nervous about meeting you, but I assured him that you would wish us well."

"And I do," I said. And I meant it. Mostly. "We do have odd timing, don't we?"

"Believe me, I've noticed," John said.

"Will you come to dinner on Friday?" I asked.

"Of course," John said. "Will you come to Provincetown in September?"

"I want to," I said. Which was more or less the truth. "I'll have to figure it out. My stupid job, and all."

"So you won't come," John said, looking slightly deflated. "We've always been honest with each other, haven't we? Please don't bullshit me now."

I pulled myself together, and said, "Of course I'll come. How could I not? How could I not give away the most lovable man in the world to his perfect mate?"

"So I can stop holding my breath?" John asked.

"Yes," I said. "It's bad for your digestion."

"My parents are looking forward to seeing you, too."

"Is that the truth?—John Alegria, you are too much for words." And he was. When Brian returned to the table we were giggling about something outrageous Bunny Babbit said, in Provincetown, the summer of '76: "Fucking is like gambling: you have to be in it to win it." We filled Brian in on the joke, and the three of us had a good laugh together. And then we moved on to a good dinner together. The three of us. Nothing was what I had anticipated. But it was all good.

I was working on Thursday and Friday, so I spent Thursday evening planning and shopping for our Friday dinner. It had to be simple, but I wanted it to be festive as well. *Salumi,* and some salady things that I could make ahead, to start. I went to my neighborhood shop with the best *prosciutto* and *soppressata,* and while I was at it, I bought some marinated artichoke hearts, and *caponata.* All I would have to make was an arugula salad with cherry tomatoes and sliced boiled eggs, and half the meal was set.

For the main course, I decided to bake a whole bluefish using a recipe John gave me all those years before from his grandmother's food journal. Lemon, garlic, parsley, and olive oil, mostly, with lots of cracked black pepper on the skin. Perfect. And I could serve it just warm, in case the air conditioning was not at its best.

Marcia Grace was still my roommate. Marcia had a dinner date, but I invited her to have a glass of wine with us before she headed out, and she accepted. The boys arrived, we seated them, and poured some wine. I had decided on a rosé. From the south of France, I think. Today I would proudly serve one from Portugal, but in those years the Portuguese wines—other than porto—that made it to New York and most other parts of the US were mostly of the pop variety, like those silly imports in the 1960s.

We started our evening. Marcia was a lot of fun, and she enjoyed meeting John and Brian. I was in the kitchen, slipping the fish into the oven, when Marcia announced that she was off to her date. She stopped by the kitchen. "They're *cute!*" Marcia told me *sotto voce*, on her way out.

"John is maybe my oldest friend," I said.

"And you let him get away?"

"It's complicated," I said.

"Uh-huh," Marcia said. "Gotta run!"

The three of us headed to the table. "I can't believe I have two handsome men tonight, one on either side of me," I said.

"Yes, but which one gets to sit at your right hand?" John asked.

"I can't choose. I think you'd better flip for it," I said. And they did. Brian won the toss and took his place on my right. "Don't worry," I said to John. "I'm left handed. So I won't neglect you." Dinner was delightful. The fish was perfectly done, if I do say so myself. And the rest of it was just fine. We ate and laughed and said silly things. I truly wanted to make

Brian feel welcome. I hope I did. I had been in his shoes in the past, and I wanted to smooth his way.

After coffee and a few bites of a very rich chocolate torte I bought—nice but nothing like the ones I used to bake, back when I had the leisure to bake them— it really was time for our little evening to end. The guys had early morning plans, and I had to go to work. We stirred from our post-dinner torpor and started the going-home ritual.

John thanked me first. "How could you remember Granny's baked fish? No one else makes it anymore. You're a remarkable man."

"I understand why John loves you," Brian said. "Thanks for a wonderful dinner."

I embraced Brian, gave him a big kiss, and quietly warned him, "John is the best man I've ever known, and if you hurt him, I'll flay you alive." Brian managed a promise and a chuckle. A lesser man would have harrumphed or frozen like a deer in the headlights. But Brian stood his ground, and then said, "Don't forget, Provincetown in September. If you don't come, we'll call the whole thing off."

"I'll be there," I said.

"I'll head out to First Avenue to look for a cab," Brian said.

"Thank you, Bri," John said. "I'll be right out."

John and I were really alone together for the first time in more than fifteen years. "Well, we don't have time for this," John said, "but I have to tell you that you were the first man who took my heart. And you will always keep a big piece of it."

Perhaps I was feeling noble. Perhaps I had achieved a bit of maturity. Not bloody likely. But whatever my motives, instead of going wacko I simply said, "Don't keep Brian waiting. He deserves your undivided attention."

"Yes."

"Could I have a kiss?" I asked.

"Yes."

And I took my prize—not so much "A Kiss to Build a Dream On" as a gentle reminder that the most lovable man in the world loved *me*. For whatever reasons. And then he was gone.

Would I go to Provincetown in September and give John away? I'd have to, I supposed. I'd given my word, after all. Could I do it with an open, unselfish heart? I'd have to, I supposed. And where would I find an open, unselfish heart? Maybe I could grow one, I decided. In about two months? Hey, you never know.

# Chapter Sixteen

**A hot guy named Bradley** used to cut my hair, years ago. He worked in a salon just up First Avenue. Not only was he a great hair-cutter—with some A-List clients (one of whom does regular fund-raising pitches on PBS)—but he was also very sweet. The cuts were great, the chats even better. We talked dirty, and he used to have some stories to tell, indeed. This was in a simpler, safer time, though the storm clouds were already forming. It was the early '80s.

One afternoon I walked upstairs to the little corner salon with the wrap-around windows, and there was Bradley with his knees on the window banquette, his elbows on the windowsill, and his exceptionally cute butt facing the door as I walked in. The sight of those denim-clad cheeks is burned indelibly into my memory. I had to greet Bradley—without groping him, as much as I might have wanted to—before he said to me, without turning around, "Look at that." "That" was the guy across the street standing in the doorway of the little pharmacy. It was the first time I noticed Henry Tauber in the neighborhood.

Tauber. Hmm. It's a river, you know. I had a vague sense of that, not that I could have placed it on a map of Europe. But I do, after all, have this thing about water. And he looked familiar, even though I was certain we had never met. I already told you he was someone we knew slightly. After Bradley's "introduction," I dropped by the pharmacy occasionally, to pick up a bottle of peroxide or a new toothbrush. That's all young people really need from a pharmacy. I could have gotten those things cheaper at a chain store, but I liked seeing Henry. And flirting with him. He was tall, and reed-thin, with what used to be called a "distinguished" look. His dark hair and beard were shot with white—or, as Horatio described Hamlet's father, "a sable sil-ver'd"—and they framed a face that was lean and full of character. In other words, he was a perfect fantasy. Had I not been partnered? Had he not been partnered? Who knows?

Our relationship was not entirely limited to those occasional, semi-professional interactions at the pharmacy. There were chance meetings at the supermarket, too. Henry told me years later that he used to drop into D'Ag's before work for something he didn't really need, on the chance he might encounter me. And since I shopped nearly every day for school or for my home kitchen, the chances were good.

Henry came to the apartment for dinner one evening when we needed an "extra man" and he was available. He was a delightful guest. Bobby liked him very much. And so did our other guests. Henry knew a lot about dance (because of his partner), and theater (because of his partner), and New York, because he was a smart New Yorker—NYU, Columbia. And I watched him charm the barnacles off a particularly crusty woman who had been difficult all evening long.

She melted during the dessert course—please don't ask me what I served, because it was nothing to do with the food. It was just that Henry assured her that her doubts about her doctor's advice were probably well founded. And that she should trust her own instincts. And maybe get another opinion. By the time we got to coffee and cordials, she wanted his card. I loved having Henry in our home. I also loved—even more, I think—his good-night kiss. "May I call you Hank?" I asked. "I don't think I've ever had a Hank in my life."

"Yes, of course," he answered. He phoned the next day to thank us for dinner. That was normal life in those days. I thanked him for his call as I felt a big twitch in my groin. That was also normal life, for me, anyway. A week or two later, Hank invited *us* to dinner, but the date didn't work for us. And then we were all caught up in the swirl of life, and then years went by and we had only a wave or a brief chat, or a brief flirtation when we happened to meet in the neighborhood. I loved running into Hank, partly because he was deadly attractive, and partly because he was attracted to me. And yet? Hank knew no more about our journey, really, than we did about his.

And then as the summer of 1992 was winding down, and Bobby and I were preparing to separate, we learned that Hank's mate had just died. I told you about the condolence note. Bobby was the one who said, "Hank's a quality guy. He deserves our sympathy." I didn't have the heart to tell Hank that Bobby's and my relationship had also died. I simply went into polite autopilot and said the right things—I hoped. Politely.

Hank replied and invited us to a memorial service. I had never met Hank's mate, not to mention that I had developed a fierce allergy to memorials. Bobby was already starting his new life. I declined. Respectfully. For both of us. But Hank did not disappear from my consciousness.

In October I phoned him and suggested we meet for supper at a little Indian restaurant in the neighborhood. He accepted. To be perfectly honest, I called Hank mostly because I already knew him. We had already done the flirting dance. What I had in mind was not being alone, of course, and also some quick, uncomplicated sex that did not require a whole lot of dating foreplay.

Our Indian dinner was fun. We chatted easily about this and that, neighborhood stuff, New York stuff. I told what I could bear to repeat about the last months and the breakup. He told me about his partner's last hospitalization. "I realized I didn't have a decent black suit," Hank said, "and that I would soon need one. My only chance to go shopping was right after work, my usual time for visiting Steve. And he looked forward to my visits all day. I couldn't tell him what I was doing, of course, so I had to invent a story for why I was so late." A shared sense of deep loss gave us much in common.

"You know, Steve was not my first love. I was married once, did I ever tell you that?"

"No, I don't think so," I said.

"Well, we don't really know each other very well, do we?"

"No, not very."

"I'd like to change that," Hank said.

"So would I," I said.

After dinner, Hank came to the apartment—my place, now—and I led him to my new bed. The featherbed I loved so. He didn't tell me until much later that he hated that bed. But he joined me there anyway. *Hmm, this feels like making love,* I thought, *and sober too.* And you know what? It was lovemaking! All I had expected was hot sex. But there was much more than mere sex happening that evening in my cozy featherbed.

We met another time or two that fall. We both sensed, I think, that something important might be happening. But we both were suddenly single after years of being partnered—nearly seventeen for each of us—and there was no point in rushing into something new. No. No rushing. Time to heal. Time to adjust. Time to get our selves back.

Hank invited me to his Christmas party. Or maybe it was a Chanukah party. Whatever. Spending holidays alone was a new and unpleasant experience, so I was more than happy to accept his invitation. Big, soft persimmons were particularly good that season, so I decided to bake a persimmon pudding. I hadn't encountered such a thing since my Southern childhood, but I was able to find a recipe. God bless the Rombauers and the Beckers. The pudding looked right, and it smelled right, so I was proud to take it along.

One of Hank's guests was a very tall guy named Dennis, who took an interest in me. We talked for a while, and flirted a bit. I thought he was interesting. Much later, Hank told me that Dennis phoned him the next day with thanks and said, "That persimmon pudding was really good, but not as sweet as the guy who brought it. Would you mind giving me his phone number?"

Hank thought about it, and then said, "I would, actually." That was Hank's aha moment. And mine? I think it came the following month when we had dinner to celebrate his birthday. We went to a welcoming little pasta joint in his neighborhood. I brought a bottle of red wine. The food was good. We had a good time. And then we went to Hank's apartment and made love. If I didn't know before, I certainly knew by the end of that lovely evening. But really, a new relationship so soon after the last one failed? No. Out of the question.

And yet, we did see each other. Often. That spring. Into the summer. We shared dinners, went to the theater—lots of off-Broadway—and dance concerts occasionally. Museums, flea markets. We even took the Circle Line cruise around Manhattan, without a single out-of-town guest in tow, simply because we decided we deserved it.

By August, at least, I knew that we were "in a relationship." As much as I had determined not to go there. We were sharing dinner one evening when I said, "An old friend asked me to stand up for him at his commitment ceremony, next month."

"How nice is that?" Hank said.

"Very nice, except that it's in Provincetown."

"Provincetown is beautiful! Hank said. I was only there once, and that was a long time ago."

"Me, too," I said. "I didn't know what to tell him."

"I hope you told him yes," Hank said.

"More or less."

"Why are you so hesitant?"

"Because I was once madly in love with John, and now he's asked me to give him away. It seems so final."

"You don't suppose you'll have to do a little growing up, do you?" Hank asked.

"You think?"

"I'm sure you'll rise to the occasion."

"Thanks for the vote of confidence," I said. "I haven't asked for the time off yet. I guess it won't be such a big deal. It's not like it's during the Christmas season or anything like that. I'll only need four days for the trip: two regular days off and two vacation days. I'll arrange it tomorrow."

"Good," Hank said. "And now maybe you'll enjoy your dinner."

I had only been picking at my food, as Hank noticed, and it was double-sautéed pork at my favorite neighborhood Chinese. Once the decision was entirely made, I relaxed and enjoyed my dinner and our evening together. "Will you miss me while I'm away?" I asked.

"I always miss you when we're apart," Hank said.

"Is that the truth?" I asked.

"Of course," Hank said.

"Good to know." I said. And it *was* good to know. I hadn't quite wrapped my brain around the concept of being half of a couple again. Could I do it?

## Chapter Seventeen

**It would have been fun** to stay at the Pilgrim House again. But John informed me that it had burned to the ground three years before, taking a whole lot of memories with it, of course, including my own. John suggested I stay at a little guest house whose owner was an old friend of his. The rate, after Labor Day, was half that of the high season. And there was a special discount for the wedding guests. Perfect. On travel day, the train to Boston arrived a few minutes early, and I made it to the ferry in plenty of time.

It only takes ninety minutes to cross Cape Cod Bay, yet another world waits on the far shore. It's the marine scent, I think, that always gets me. It bathes my senses the moment the boat moves into open water and the diesel fumes are swept away. Provincetown began to work its magic on me even before John waved to me from the ferry dock on Mac-Millan Pier, as we were pulling in. We disembarked. "Thank you *so much* for coming," John said as he hugged me.

"Enough of that!" I said. "I couldn't have said no."

"Give me that bag," John said. "I'll walk you to the guest house. It's only a few blocks." We linked our free arms and set out. It was, indeed, a short walk. "Mom and Dad want you to come to dinner this evening," John said.

"That's so kind of them. Of course. I'd love to," I said.

"I think dinner will be at 7:00, but why not come early, about 6:00? Brian is looking forward to seeing you, too."

"I'll put my itinerary in your very handsome, very capable hands." I said.

"So you're mine for the next two days?" John asked.

"I've been yours for the last seventeen years. You never noticed?" I asked.

"We somehow missed most of them, didn't we? But let's get you checked in." And so we did. And then John walked me to my room. "We've tried to keep it simple, but things tend to escalate when there are more than two people involved, as I'm sure you know."

"Tell me," I said.

"The service is at 1:00 tomorrow, at the Universalist Church. I'll meet you here at noon, just to make sure we have plenty of time. And then we can walk over together."

"Great."

"Heidi and Liz insisted on giving us a reception at the gallery afterward. I didn't want them to go to all that trouble, but I had to say yes. Cliff will be there. He's looking forward to seeing you," John said.

"Cliff's a pistol," I said.

"He adores you."

"The feeling is mutual," I said.

"Well, I'll let you relax. About 6:00? Can I give you the address?" John asked.

"I could find it in my sleep. As indeed I have, on many occasions. But that was your little apartment in the old stable in the back. Still, I'm sure I can navigate to the front door."

"I almost forgot!" John said. "There's a little rehearsal at 5:00 at the church. Just you and me and Brian and his friend Carl. And the minister, of course. It won't take long. And then we'll walk over together."

"Even better," I said. John hugged me and started to thank me, again. I stopped that with a kiss. And then he left me to settle into my room. It was a charming room, a bit small but perfect for one. It was furnished in soft shades of blue and beige with just enough bits of "nauticalia" here and there to make the room feel site-specific, but not so much that it fell into kitsch. I tested the bed, and it felt very inviting indeed. I unpacked a little and hung up my wedding suit. And then I took a nap.

I made it to the church exactly at 5:00. The boys got there before me. I greeted John first, of course, and then Brian, who seemed even cuter than I remembered. "Thank you so much for coming!" Brian said. "I want you to meet my best friend, Carl Smithers." Carl flashed me an easy grin, and we embraced, even though we were meeting for the first time. *Hmm*, I thought, *He smells good! And a redhead. Always inviting. This trip may turn out to be more fun than I expected.*

I had never entered the sanctuary at the Universalist Church. There's nothing like these old Unitarian meeting houses anywhere outside of New England, as far as I know. I was expecting Shaker austerity, and instead I was greeted by a surprisingly ornate interior with crystal chandeliers, organ pipes, and rich woodwork—all very linear, though, with scarcely a curlicue in sight. Did I decide to join? No, but it was tempting.

The pastor arrived shortly after I did, wearing a sweatshirt that said "God doesn't discriminate. Neither do we." I liked her instantly. The warmth of her smile was contagious, and I could feel the love and acceptance she exuded—just what we all want in a religious leader and so rarely get. We got right to our rehearsal: The boys were instructed to walk in from the front of the church after the congregation was all seated and the music announced the start of the ceremony.

Luckily there were niches off the entryway where Carl and I could wait, with our grooms, until the processional. John and I would be house-right and Brian and Carl house-left. Carl and I were to follow the boys in and then flank them at the altar. The minister went through the order of the service, so Carl and I would know when to do our bit, when to retreat a few steps, and when to produce the rings.

*I think I can handle this*, I thought. *Maybe after a good night's sleep I won't be so nervous,* I hoped. Yeah, sure.

It was a beautiful evening as we walked to the Alegrias' house. "Tomorrow is supposed to be just as nice," John said. "Let's hope." I had never been to the main house, only the little stable in back. I didn't dare look at that. I knew without being told that John and Brian were staying there. And I was unable to manage even a glance.

Mr. and Mrs. Alegria greeted us at the front door. John's dad, Bill, was looking a good bit older, of course, but still hot. He was obviously the source of much of John's beauty—his glowing skin, and black hair, and great smile. I sensed that John had a whole lot more years of handsome to look forward to. Bill said, "John was really looking forward to your arrival, and so were we. Welcome!"

Joan Alegria was more reserved, but also welcoming. I didn't know whether to expect an embrace, and I wouldn't have initiated one. But Joan embraced me, very simply and naturally. "I'm so happy to see you again!" I said.

"We didn't know when you'd get up this way again. John says you're still living in New York," she said.

"Yes, and I'm so glad this occasion brings us together. I loved seeing you at the greenmarket that summer. Are you still there?"

"No, I gave it up last year. Too much work, I guess. I miss it, but not those early mornings," she said.

"Well, it was my favorite place to shop, and I've never forgotten the time John and I went there together. You were so kind to us. Anyway, it's good to be back." I said.

"Bill and I are delighted you're here. Let him pour you a glass of wine, and I need to look in on some things in the kitchen, if you'll excuse me."

"Of course," I said. The house was charming, a perfect blend of Yankee and Iberian sensibilities— pure Cape Cod. Bill did pour me a glass of wine and directed me to a very comfortable chair. We menfolk talked and laughed and drank wine while Joan made all the preparations, with just a bit of help from a woman who worked for them occasionally.

And then Joan pulled off that amazing magic act that women have performed for ages—she sat us down at a table set with good linen, good silver, good china, and good crystal and then served a delicious dinner for six while making the whole thing look effortless. I knew better, of course. I told her as much. Hosts deserve all the praise they can get.

We took coffee in the living room. "Who's nervous about tomorrow?" Bill asked.

"I am!" said all four of us boys in unison.

"Don't be," Bill said. "Just be ready to say 'I do' whenever they ask a question."

"Bill, I seem to remember that before our wedding, I was afraid we might have to peel you off the ceiling," Joan said.

"That was a long time ago," Bill said, "but I made the right decision, and I've never regretted a moment of it."

It was a lovely dinner, and then it was time to leave. The grooms were staying in the little apartment in back—surprise, surprise—and Carl was headed a few blocks farther west to stay with a friend. After thank-yous and good-byes, John walked me out to the street. "Let me give you the ring before I forget," he said.

"Of course." I stuffed it in my pocket. "John, I'm so happy for you!" I said, with a high degree of honesty.

"And I'm most happy tonight that you're here," he said. "Get some rest, Old Friend, and I'll see you at noon."

I headed back without a single glance toward the old stable. I did, however, glance at the ring on my way back to the hotel. It was perfect: just an endless band of gold. I considered trying it on, but only for an instant. Even I am not creepy enough to do something like that. How could I send my old friend into his new life with a tarnished token? No, it would have been terrible karma. I stowed the ring in my pocket and headed to the hotel.

John arrived at my room just before noon. I was nearly dressed, mostly just shirt and tie to go. John looked terrific, of course. And he smelled so good that I felt myself in danger of backing out. "I'm calling room service," John said. "Should we have a coffee, or maybe a brandy?"

"Your call. Maybe both?"

John placed the order and then said, "I feel a little selfish. This day is all about *my* happiness, and what about yours?"

"Don't be ridiculous," I said. "My happiness has nothing to do with it."

"You never told me what happened with you and Bobby."

"Other than a great sea of vodka coming between us, there's not all that much to tell. I survived the flood, and so did he."

"That sounds like the *Reader's Digest* version."

"And so it is. And that's all you'll get from me today. This is only about you." I was fumbling with cuff links. John stepped over to help.

"You mentioned that you've been seeing someone," John said. "Talk to me. We have time before we need to leave. And I don't think they'll start without us." John finished putting the links in my cuffs and then took both my hands in his.

127

"I love my new life," I said. "Don't get me wrong. I'm not complaining. It's just that I feel a bit cheated. I don't even know your body," I said. "I only know the version of it that I've imagined for all these years. I wanted. . ."

"So did I."

"I wanted . . ."

"So did I."

"I wanted you inside me. I wanted me inside you. I wanted to kiss you so deeply that we lost all boundaries. I wanted to lie next to you and lose myself in your warmth and the scent of your hair. I wanted to feel your arms envelope me. I wanted to kiss your feet. I wanted to worship you. I'd have gladly spent a lifetime on my knees before you. I wanted to *be* you, and for *you* to be *me*. I wanted it all. And I wanted it to be forever."

"Thank you for your honesty," John said. "You deserve the same. The truth is, I wanted everything you wanted. Maybe more. I wanted to wake up every morning with your breath on my face. I wanted to exchange pillows so that I could smell you all night long. I wanted to stay up much too late at night laughing and making love because I couldn't bear the thought of *not* laughing and making love with you."

"John, we don't really need to have this conversation."

"Of course we do. You've wanted it as much as I have."

"More, perhaps. But, today?"

"Did I imagine us in a cottage on a lake in New Hampshire with a kerosene stove and flannel shirts and a golden retriever? Yes. Did I imagine us in a walk-up apartment on the North End with suppers of takeout fried oysters and coleslaw? Yes. Did I imagine us building a life in Boston together and then going home to Provincetown for a few weeks every summer? Yes. Did I imagine moving to New York, simply because it was where you wanted to live? Yes."

"John, this is. . ."

"It's the truth."

"Yes. And since we're on that topic: Did I imagine leaving Bobby and running away to you? Yes. Did I imagine us living in that sweet little apartment in the old stable behind your parents' house? Yes. Would I have been willing to release you from that old brass bed? Never. If you had asked me to leave Bobby when we had lunch at Jacob Wirth in the fall of 1986—which you did not—would I have left him? We'll never know. I'm sorry, John. This is your wedding day. I've been ridiculous, I know."

"No. We have every right to say these things. They should have been said years ago. But they weren't. So we're saying them now. If you had been available, I would have built my life around you. But you weren't available. And that's a fact of life."

"Yes."

"I love Brian."

"Of course you do," I said. "He's quite nearly as lovable as you are."

"It's different. But just as sweet. Will you let me keep your love as I move into this new life?"

"Only if you accept an increase. John Alegria, you have astounded me since the day we met. And I have never loved you more than I do at this very minute."

"I couldn't do this without you."

"You can do anything, John. But I'm glad you want me to be a part of it."

The room service waiter arrived with our coffees and our brandies. We thanked him and tried the beverages. And took some deep breaths.

"I guess it's that time. Do you have the ring?" John asked.

"Of course," I said, anxiously patting the pocket where I had intended to stow it.

"Shall we?"

"Give me a second," I said as I searched for the ring. Surely I had put it in the inside breast pocket of my suit jacket. But it wasn't there. The side pockets? Neither one. The pants pockets? I tried all four without success.

"I gave it to you last night after dinner, didn't I?" John asked.

"Yes, and I thought I put it away as soon as I got back to the room. Or did I. . . Let me just check my jeans," which were hanging on a hook in the closet. I held my breath and searched the pockets, one at a time, starting with the left front. When I got to the last one, the right front, I was nearly frantic. And then I struck gold. The sense of relief was physical. I took another deep breath and chugged the last of my brandy. And then we headed to the church.

# Chapter Eighteen

**It really was a lovely ceremony.** The pastor had suggested a service for John and Brian to consider. They accepted most of it and added a few ideas of their own. They also wrote their own vows, which had become a very popular option. "Dearly beloved," the welcome began, and we were off and running.

I was quite touched by an early part of the ceremony where the pastor spoke of the importance of family in the lives of the new couple. She said, "Mr. and Mrs. Alegria," who were seated in the front row aisle seats behind us, "Will you accept Brian into your family and love him as your own son?"

To which they responded, of course, "We will."

"Mr. And Mrs. Mathews," who were seated behind Brian and Carl, "Will you accept John into your family and love him as your own son?"

"We will."

And then the entire gathering was asked to voice their support for the new couple, and of course we all said, loudly and in unison, "We will."

And then came my bit: The pastor asked, "Who vouches for John, for his honesty and his worthiness to be joined today in love to Brian?"

"I do," I said.

"Who vouches for Brian, for his honesty and his worthiness to be joined today in love to John?"

"I do," Carl said. And then Carl and I stepped back a bit, because we had served our main function. *I did it,* I thought. *I gave him away. At least I got to say "I do."*

The vows were lovely. Most of it's a swirl in my memory, but I'm certain I heard John say, "Brian, you fill my heart with such joy that I want to share my life with you. I want us to experience both the good and the bad together. And I pledge to respect you and support you and love you completely as long as I live."

Carl and I produced the rings on cue, of course. There were a few little announcements, including an invitation to the reception, and then it was time to finish: "Inasmuch as John and Brian have come together today, in the presence of their loved ones, and declared their intentions, with the power vested in me by God and this congregation, I now pronounce you joined in love. You may seal your bond with a kiss." And they did. Deeply.

The music swelled, and it was time to leave. The boys went first, of course, followed by Carl and me. And then it was out the front door and into the afternoon sunlight. The weather couldn't have been nicer, and I was feeling quite buoyant. The parents were the next ones out of the meeting house, and then the rest of the guests. Quite soon I saw Cliff steering his way toward me with an exceptionally pretty young woman on his arm. "Please meet Alicia. She already knows you're my favorite uncle," Cliff said.

"I'm so happy to meet you," Alicia said, extending her hand. She was even prettier up close, and very sweet. She was dressed in sheer silk—*How do women walk around practically naked?* I wondered—

with just a charming little brocaded shawl draped over her shoulders against the late summer chill coming in from the bay.

"So you know he's my favorite nephew," I said.

"I suspected it."

"Well, it's all true," I said, taking her aside. "But that doesn't mean he can do no wrong. Does he treat you well?"

"Yes, I think so," Alicia said, looking slightly puzzled.

"And will you tell me if that changes?"

"If you want."

"Don't mind me, Alicia. I think you're delightful, and I couldn't be happier to see Cliff in love. He is in love, you know. It's unmistakable. And you'll be very kind to each other, I hope."

"Yes." Alicia was more than ready to escape my grilling, so I kissed her on both pretty cheeks and sent her off to greet her friends.

"Why, Cliff, I do declare you've grown even more handsome than when last we met," I said. "How did you manage that?"

"Magic," Cliff said.

"That Bunny," I said. "I'd stick with him if I were you,"

"I intend to. And by the way, you're looking pretty good yourself," Cliff said.

"Weddings bring out the best in everyone. You'll let me know when it's your turn?" I said. "I wouldn't want to miss it."

"Would you give me away?" Cliff asked.

"Only to the perfect woman," I said. "Your family—all of us—expect nothing less than perfection for you. And *from* you. So when you're ready, you'll tell me. And I'll drop everything to be there."

"Why are you so kind to me?" Cliff asked.

"Because your father and your mothers were kind to *me* at a point in my life when I was less mature, emotionally, than even you are, if you can imagine that. And because I think you're stellar. And because I love you more than I have any right to, even more than I could if you were my own son. Does that answer your question?"

"You're going to make me cry.

"Hell, it's a wedding. Why not!"

"What about our date?" Cliff asked.

"What date?": I asked.

"In three years," Cliff said.

"I thought that was an 'if,' " I said.

"I thought it was a 'when.' " he said.

"So you think we should put it on the calendar? Your eighteenth birthday?"

"In red letters."

"Do you think I'll still be able to get it up in three years?" I asked.

"I think you'll still be getting it up in *fifty* years. I hope I'm around to see it," Cliff said.

"I hope so, too. Let me just say this, Young Man: I'm available. I'm always available for love-making. I won't make that mistake again—not being available. And I don't want you to do that either!"

"Yes, Sir!"

"And don't call me sir!"

"Yessir."

"Run along and play, Cliff. Alicia is waiting for you." I kissed him and sent him on his way. Did I also shed a few tears? Of course. But nothing I couldn't handle.

Heidi and Liz had already headed to the gallery to finish the preparations for the reception, and Anita and Moises were the only other wedding guests I really wanted to see. "I can't believe I'm getting to see you twice in one year. How are you?" I asked as I embraced Anita.

"The better for seeing you again. Sunny, I have to say, you're as handsome as the grooms."

"And that's high praise indeed, isn't it?"

Moises greeted me next. His bear hug was less powerful than I remembered, though no less sincere. Moises looked smaller and grayer, but totally himself. I hadn't even realized how much I had missed seeing him. "Could we have a meal together before I leave?" I asked.

"We were thinking of dinner, tomorrow," Anita said. "Does that work for you?"

"Perfect," I said.

"I'm going to cook for you." Anita said.

"Please, Anita. You don't have to do that! We should go out."

"But I want to. Come at 6:00 and we'll have a good visit."

"But Anita, it's too much work!" I said.

Moises said, "Sunny, you know better than to argue with Anita once she's made up her mind."

"Quite right. 6:00 then. Thank you!"

The gallery was just as I remembered it—neat, whitewashed, scrubbed pine flooring. It was also more alive than I had ever seen it. There were tables with great trays of food and a bar with plenty of bubbly chilling in a big vat of ice. All of this I observed, of course, but my eye was first drawn to the wonderful little portrait of Heath that still held a special, altarlike place of honor. I wondered if I could bear to live with his image as a daily reminder of his loss.

Liz called to me from the bar, and I was pleased to join her and give her a kiss. "Here, have a glass," she said. "You look fabulous! I think John was a little nervous about whether you'd show up or not. I told Heidi you'd be here. And Cliff was also worried. He was very excited about seeing you again."

"Liz, you give perfect party!" I said. "And I'm thrilled to be back. This is really lovely, what you've done for John and Brian. And about that son of yours . . ." And we both started to giggle. "He's a precious commodity," I said.

"We think so," Liz said.

"Well, there's no question about it, and I hope I get to see all of you more often in the future. Maybe you'll visit New York every year or so?"

"Or maybe you'll come back to Provincetown without waiting another sixteen years!" Liz said.

"Touché!" I said. "Where's Heidi? I've hardly seen her all day."

"She's right over there, talking to Anita and Moises." And so she was.

"I'll peel off and leave you to sling your booze in peace," I said. "Liz, this has been such a treat for me, being back here. I'll be in town tomorrow, but I'm not sure if I'll see you or not. Anyway, we'll talk. I love you." I kissed her good-bye and headed to where my other friends were gathered. "Heidi, you've been hiding from me all day!" I said. I embraced her and felt an uncharacteristically warm response. Heidi had always seemed enigmatic to me: full of Nova Scotian reserve and lesbian spine, and yet surprisingly gentle at the oddest moments. "Great party," I said. "Look at Liz: she's still party central!"

"We're all so glad you could make it," Heidi said. "It wouldn't have been the same without you."

"I'm glad I made it, too," I said. "I told Liz, I'm not so sure about tomorrow. I know Anita and Moises are going to attempt to overstuff me at dinnertime—and succeed, no doubt—but during the day, I'm not sure. But we'll talk."

"Yes, please."

"Heidi, it's a *really* lovely party. Thanks again." And then I headed out for a cigarette. Another reveler in search of a cigarette was Brian's friend Carl. He really was hot stuff. Did I consider hitting on him? Of course. When love is in the air all sorts of things can happen. Did I actually do it? Well, yes. We shared a smoke just around the corner from the gallery, and then I kissed him. And he kissed me back. It was great fun.

"Would you like to go out for a lobster roll, or something?" Carl asked.

"I'd love it," I said. "I think we're off duty now, but let me check."

"Yes, let me say good-bye to the boys," Carl said. We did all our good-byes and then headed to a restaurant/bar near the pier that was always fun. We ordered beer and lobster rolls. And we laughed and talked and flirted and kissed and grabbed each other and kissed a bit more. Did I invite him back to my room? No. Would he have accepted the invitation, had it been offered? I think, yes.

But in the end, I decided to return to my hotel room, alone. Don't ask me why. I've never quite figured out why I put on the brakes with a charming, handsome, hot, available man—about my age—who

had been vetted by trusted sources. And yet I did.
And I nestled into that very comfy bed, watched an
hour of TV, and then slept like a baby.

The next morning I woke late and ordered a room
service breakfast. The free time felt luxurious. I gave
Hank a call, to tell him I missed him. He was at work
and couldn't really talk, but we agreed to meet for
dinner the following evening. After a leisurely
shower, I headed out to wander around town. There
were so many memories. And Provincetown seemed
exactly the same and yet quite different. I even went
to the Pilgrim Monument—and climbed it! That was
something I never did the summer I lived there. But
now that I was just another tourist, I decided to correct that oversight.

At 4:00 I met John and Brian at the Portuguese
Bakery, for old times' sake. The *malasadas* (dough-
nuts) were just as tempting as ever, but I didn't dare
spoil my appetite for Anita's dinner. The coffee was
good, and the company better.

The newlyweds thanked me for my service, and
gave me a gift—a little gold heart to add to my neck
chain. From Doris's One of a Kind, of course. I was
touched and grateful. We strung it on my chain immediately, and I liked the feel of it on my chest. And
then it was nearly time to head to Anita and Moises's.

The three of us spilled out onto Commercial
Street. It was summer, it was fall, it was afternoon,
it was evening, it was that in-between time when it's
always lovely to have companions. We were all

headed west, and I managed to steer Brian a little bit apart from John.

"John told you we never made love?" I asked.

"Yes."

"And he told you why?"

"That you were never available."

"Precisely! Please, Brian, promise you won't make that mistake. Please, cherish him and be fully present in his life," I said.

"I promise. And thanks again for coming. It means so much to John. And to me."

"Careful, Brian!" I said, "or you may have another conquest on your hands."

"I'll take that risk," Brian said.

John embraced me one last time. "Many thanks, Old Friend," he said, "and have an easy trip home."

"John," I said. "I wouldn't have missed this for the world." And since we had left nothing unsaid, it was time to part. I wouldn't see them again that trip. I would be off on the early morning ferry, heading back to my real life. We continued west on Commercial Street until it was time for me to peel off and stop at a wine shop for a little dinner token. I lingered in the doorway of the shop for a moment, and they both turned back with a wave, and then the parting was final. I bought a bottle of wine—Portuguese, of course—and headed on.

## Chapter Nineteen

**Moises greeted me at the door.** "Come in," he said, and pulled me into another of his very welcoming, very reassuring embraces. "Anita's in the kitchen, of course. Let's join her."

"Perfect," I said. I followed Moises to the kitchen, and everything was just as I remembered it, from the blue-and-white tiles to the big refrigerator to the old range and the double sink. But, of course, it was the big old pine table in the center of the room that really drew me in. Anita was in the middle of some dinner preparations on the near end, but she had arranged place settings for the three of us at the far end.

I was so glad! It would have seemed odd to be in the "formal dining room," as if we were no longer close. Anita greeted me and put a glass of Madeira in my hand, and the years melted away. Had I really learned to pick up an old friendship where we left off, as Bobby did so well? Had I learned anything from my seventeen years with Bobby?

"I think it's going to be a lovely sunset," Anita said. "Why don't we sit in the garden for a bit. Unless the fog rolls in, of course. Let's give it a try." We took our glasses and the bottle of Madeira, and Anita brought out a big plate of *petiscos*—Portuguese *tapas*, more or less. I remember grilled octopus—a great favorite of mine—and roasted vegetables and some little shrimps that were spiced in an unfamiliar way. Tiny squid stuffed with rice and peas.

"What did you do to this *linguiça*," I asked.

"I flambéed it in *aguardente*—high-proof rum, more or less," she said in response to my puzzled look. We sat with our food and drink, quite contentedly and rather quietly, until the lovely sunset that Anita had predicted did indeed fill the western sky, and then we headed inside.

I grabbed Anita on my way in the door, swept here into my arms, and said, "You shouldn't do this."

"Shut up!" she said. So that was the end of my protest. I knew dinner would start with *caldo verde*: The shredded collards were on her cutting board when I arrived. And since it only takes a minute to finish the soup once the potato and *chouriço* base is at the boil, Moises and I sat at the table right away, and then Anita served the soup a minute later. It was perfect, of course. And just as she had taught me to make it all those years before.

Moises opened the wine I brought and declared it was a favorite of his. And I was delighted to hear it, whether that was the absolute truth or not. I was fairly quiet at dinner, for me, because I had a lump in my throat that I couldn't quite explain. But fortunately it didn't keep me from swallowing.

After the soup, Anita served us cod that she roasted with big splashes of olive oil and white wine, lots of garlic, bay leaves, parsley, and a handful of chopped tomatoes. Nothing more. Perfect. And then came a meat course! It was lamb stewed with beans, and its savor and simplicity were breathtaking. "Uncle!" I cried.

"Just a little salad," Anita said. And, of course, I was helpless to refuse. After Anita had cleared all the dinner things, I knew she would produce a sweet. And I knew I would eat it, even though I was full to bursting. I said, "I think I like Provincetown even more than I did back then. It feels more—I don't know—inclusive? More welcoming? It seems to be for everyone now, not just for Portuguese fishermen and gay boys and dyke painters."

"Interesting you should say that," Moises said. "We talk about issues like that at town meetings. And the town council is *very* much aware that our survival depends on just the kind of inclusivity—if that's a word—that you just described."

"It's a very good word, I think," I said. "Speaking of which, I loved being at the Universalist Church yesterday. I never darkened its door the whole summer I lived here."

"We don't darken church doors very often ourselves," Anita said.

"Well, but when it's time for a ritual, what can you do?" and then I had to bite my tongue, because after weddings, what do people gather for more than funerals? And there was no point in our going there. As much as Anita and Moises had gotten on with their lives, they were still much diminished by the death of their son.

As Anita brought her dessert to the table—it was an egg-yolk-rich custard with plums baked into it— she asked, "How about Cliff?"

"Don't get me started on that one," I said.

"He needs you," Anita said.

"He needs, well . . . he'll find everything he needs, I think. He's that kind of boy."

"You met Alicia?" Moises asked. "We know her grandparents. They're nice people."

"What a beauty!" I said. "I know Cliff's in love with her. That's obvious. But do you think this is it? They're so young. I'm sure I was never that young."

"I was." Anita said. "I just can't remember when. We love Heidi and Liz. And they've done a fabulous job of raising Cliff. Moises has stepped in and done some grandfatherly things through the years."

"It's not the same." Moises said. "He needs a young man in his life. He needs you."

"He needs what?"

"He needs you!" Anita said. "And he needs to be in New York."

"He's a schoolboy!" I said.

"They have schools in New York," Anita said.

"They have schools in Siberia, I'm sure, but what's that to do with me?"

"Take him in," Anita said. "Get him enrolled at Hunter. I don't know. He's a smart kid. Figure it out. Make it work."

"That's crazy!" I said.

"It's the right thing to do," Moises said.

"What would Heidi and Liz say?" I asked.

" 'Thank you!' " Anita said.

"And what would Cliff say?" I asked.

" 'Can I move in tomorrow?' " Moises said.

"He is not my child," I said as I began to weep softly.

"He could have been," Moises said. "But, no, he's Heath's child. And Heath is dead."

Anita got up from the table long enough to stop roasting me and to start roasting coffee beans.

"How could I even consider. . ."

"You'll figure it out. You're smart, too," Anita said.

"Apparently not as smart as the rest of you. Who hatched this plan?" I demanded to know.

"I did," Anita said, defiantly.

"And your co-conspirators fell right into line?" I asked.

"We did," Moises said.

"Does Cliff know about this?

"Of course not!" Anita said. "You can't just dangle children like that."

"Tell me!" I said. "But you seem to have our futures all figured out." Anita and Moises waited patiently until I was sputtered out. And then I gave them an opening: I said, "Well, I do have an apartment with an extra bedroom. And my current roommate is leaving in mid-December. But I can't afford . . ."

"Heidi and Liz would expect to pay his board." Anita said.

"This is insane."

"I think it's perfect," Anita said.

"How could I have a teenager living with me?

"Oh, yeah, like you're going to corrupt his morals," Anita said. "By next year he'll be teaching *you* things."

"Anita, I love you, but I don't quite understand what you want of me."

"I want you to take that corncob out of your ass and just accept that Cliff needs what you have to offer," Anita said. And, of course, there was no point in arguing with Anita once she had made up her mind. Moises smiled at me. It was a commiserative smile and also a proud, fatherly smile.

"If you didn't make such good coffee, I'd . . ."

"You'd what?" Anita asked.

"I'd never fall under your spell again."

145

"Well, that's okay. This one was successful, yes?" Anita asked.

"Well, yes, if I . . . I'll see. I don't know, I guess I'll look at schools as soon as I get home. This is on your head, Lady! You have to make your end happen. And would someone please ask Cliff how he feels about it, now that it's a done deal? And you'll make sure they fill out the applications and get the transcripts in the mail and all of that?" I asked.

"Yes, Nanny," Anita said.

We drank our coffee in silence. And then it was time to leave.

"I guess I threw you a curve," Anita said.

"I think it was a knuckle ball," I said.

"I'm holding to my end of our bargain," Anita said, referring to the promise she gave when she was in New York, to include me in her morning prayers.

"And I to mine," I assured her. And indeed I had developed the habit of taking a moment each morning to look at the miniature portrait of their beautiful son that she gave me all those years ago, and to hold the three of them in my heart.

When I got to the front door, Anita pressed an envelope into my hands. "Please take this sketchbook of Paul's. I think it's some of his best work. I would like to think of it as being with you. If there's a design you can use, then use it. It isn't doing anyone any good here. If there's something you can get out into the world, then do it!"

"I will, and thank you," I said. "Anita, this business with Cliff . . ."

"Will work out just fine. You'll see."

"But I don't think I can get it right. What a responsibility!" I said.

"You'll do the right thing," Anita said. "There's not a doubt in my mind. Just accept it."

*Accept it? Huh! That's easy for her to say,* I thought. But what I said was, "I'll phone as soon as I have some news. And tell Cliff he can move in in late December, if he even wants to."

"Right after Christmas should do it. That gives him a week to settle in before classes start."

"At some school or other," I said.

"You'll find the right one."

"I don't know why, Anita," I said, "but I do love you." And it was time to head out.

"Safe trip," Anita said, "and thank you."

Moises's embrace was tenderer than before. "Godspeed," he said, and I was out the door. A damp chill had rolled in from the bay. I turned up my collar and hugged myself as I made a beeline for the guesthouse. I was chilled through by the time I got back to my little room. That was more about fear than weather, of course.

How could I possibly take on this responsibility? Well, I said I was available, didn't I?

## Chapter Twenty

**Visions of Cliff** occupied my mind on the return trip, of course. The salt wind in my face on the ferry to Boston did nothing to blow away my fears. I napped as much as possible on the train. I was looking forward to dinner with Hank that evening. I had missed him, even more than I expected to. The afternoon seemed interminable.

"Well, I always said you're one hot daddy," Hank said, after I told him about the Provincetown plot.

"But Hank, let's get a little serious here," I said. "How can I have that boy living with me?"

"And why not?" Hank asked. "His mothers will pay his share of the rent, and you won't have to search for a new roommate for at least two-and-a-half years. And he's cute, you said."

"Very."

"Nice scenery is always a good thing. Relax," Hank said.

"What if I fuck this up? What if he flunks out of school? What if he becomes a drug addict?"

"You left out 'What if he gets hit by a car?' " Hank said.

"Exactly! That, too," I said.

"You do what you want," Hank said, "but I think you should just accept this and get on with it. It sounds like the kid needs you."

"Have you been talking to Anita?" I asked. " 'Accept it,' 'He needs you'—I've heard this before."

"Luckily, you have wise friends. So, it's probably too late to get him enrolled at Hunter for the January term, but what about the Cathedral School? It's right across the street, after all."

"Don't tell me you haven't been talking to Anita," I said.

"Never met the woman," Hank said.

⌕

I can't say I exactly relaxed into it, but I did walk through the process, and we got Cliff into the Cathedral School for the January term. And he moved in the day after Christmas. Cliff took to New York like a duckling to water. I stopped being *quite* so fearful and just let him get on with his life. And he did. And he studied, enough that we were able to get him accepted at Hunter for the fall term.

Cliff spent half the summer in Provincetown, of course, and I missed him horribly. Hmm, empty nest syndrome. How conventional! And then he was back and starting a new school, and before I knew it he was about to graduate. Anita was right, as usual. He got the education he needed, and I got the satisfaction of enabling his success.

And our date? As it happened, Cliff had his sexuality all figured out long before his eighteenth birthday (as Anita could have told me). He didn't need me for that. But he did need me to make a home for him—to see that he finished his homework and ate properly, and to love him. So for his eighteenth, instead of going to bed we went to dinner. And it was better.

If he had sensed that it was important to me, Cliff would probably have kept our date. That's who he is. And he might have liked it. But even if he had, it would have been not because he loves *men*, but because he loves *me*. And eighteen is hard enough without added confusions. No, I couldn't have done it, as much as I might have wanted it. Instead, I gave him the love he needed, and I've always been proud of the results.

Letting go was painful, but suddenly Cliff was off to Stanford. And he didn't need me anymore. But he stopped for a few days every summer on his way home to Provincetown. I would make up the sofa in the living room for him to sleep on, and he would stow his gear in a corner. With all the things a young man can do in New York, he would check in with a few school friends and then spend the rest of his time with me.

We went to the Metropolitan Museum. And to the Metropolitan Opera. Cliff loves Puccini; I've always been more of a Mozart man, myself. But it's all good. We went to some of Cliff's favorite restaurants, and sometimes I cooked for him. And it felt just as if he had never left home. Like picking up an old friendship where we left off, as Bobby did? Perhaps I had learned something after all.

Did I give Cliff away? Yes! His senior year at Stanford he met an extraordinary young woman and decided she was the one. And he brought her to New

York to meet me. Jennifer is beautiful, sharp as a whip, and a gifted biochemist. And she adores Cliff. So, what's not to like? Nothing, actually. They planned a wedding for August—in Provincetown, of course. I dropped everything and showed up, as I had promised. And Cliff gave me the full Father of the Groom treatment. I rarely stopped weeping the entire trip.

Anita was very much a part of the proceedings. Moises had died that winter, so she was still a bit fragile. But she showed up with vigor for all the wedding events. Anita and I had dinner together, of course. In a restaurant! And we renewed our vows of remembrance. We stepped right back into our friendship where we had left it. It was great to see Heidi and Liz, of course. And John and Brian came from Boston. It was a lovely wedding, a lovely trip, and a lovely reunion.

Cliff now works for a software company and lives in San Francisco. He and Jennifer have two children, a boy and a girl. They come to New York for two weeks every summer (except the years the kids were born). I used to be terrified of children—their honesty, I think. But these two are delightful. Perhaps I'm mellowing.

In the winter of 2008, Cliff flew to New York, alone, and the two of us went to Provincetown for Anita's funeral. It was as painful as any loss in my life, having to say good-bye to Anita. Cliff felt it too, of course, as did the moms and everyone whose life she touched. I have never missed a morning moment of remembrance of Anita and Moises and their son. It grounds me and helps me prepare for whatever the new day will bring.

Cliff never fails to phone me on Father's Day. I'll confess I text him often these days, and he always seems to find time to answer the Old Man. And he often gives me tips on new programs to try and which hardware to buy. It's good to have Silicon Valley in the family. And it's even better to have such a fine man in my life.

___

If I'm going to be honest, then I have to tell you about another funeral. A memorial, actually. This one I attended alone. Allen didn't phone to tell me Bobby died. I had to read it in *The New York Times*. Actually, I'm not much of an obituary reader, so it was a friend who read it and then phoned me—not knowing I was unaware—to offer sympathy.

It wasn't a complete shock. I had spoken to Bobby on his birthday, a few months before, so I knew he had a few mini strokes. And I also knew he had some unfortunate cardiovascular DNA from his mother. Tough to outrun. It was just that he had always been so youthful, so it just didn't quite seem real. Have I forgiven Allen for not informing me? No, not really. But I did phone him as soon as I heard, to offer sympathy. I would have had more respect for Allen's loss had he respected mine.

Allen didn't hesitate to call when he needed my help with an insurance matter—a change of beneficiary that had never been filed. I was happy to help. I tried to be gracious, but I also referred to him, once or twice, to friends, as "The Widdo' James." Sometimes flippancy seems the only way to process a situation, and I knew it was exactly what Bobby would have said, had the shoe been on another foot.

Allen did invite me to the memorial, the following year. And he asked me to speak, which was appropriate, of course. The one year's distance from the event helped me to keep my feelings at arm's length enough to get through my eulogy without incident. It was a good service, at the Players' Club. Most of Bobby's remaining living friends showed up, including my old ex-friend Kathy. A few LA people who couldn't make it sent letters for the MC to read. The guests included many former intimates of mine whom I hadn't seen in a dozen years. Words were spoken and songs sung, and it really was a lovely tribute to a remarkable man.

Those of us who were speaking were given the order of events just before the program began. Broadway crooner Andy MacGraff saw that he was to follow me and he asked, "What are you going to sing? I always want to know about the act I have to follow." We laughed, and then from the stage I ad-libbed just enough to say, "And don't worry, Andy, I'm not going to sing, so you don't have to worry about following this act."

I won't give you the text of my eulogy, but I'll share the end of it. It still feels so right to me, after all these years:

"It is an honor to be here in such wonderful company—people who loved Bobby James. I just want to say out loud, in front of God and everybody, that he was my first love, my partner, my teacher, my joy, my test-kitchen taster, my whole life at times. He gave me simple, unconditional love. I loved him so hard that sometimes it hurt. My whole life has been shaped by his gentle presence, and I wouldn't trade a moment of it. Thank you for listening."

Then, when Andy got to the podium, he addressed me directly, and said, "You're quite wrong. You're a very tough act to follow, indeed." I was touched, of course. But it was that kind of day. And it really did offer a small sense of closure.

# Chapter Twenty-one

A few weeks after I returned from Provincetown that strange summer of 1993—after having given away my old flame to his beloved and accepted, more or less, a strange new parental project—I met Hank for a bite after the gym. We went to our favorite Chinese noodle shop, on Second Avenue. Little Bit of Everything in Clear Soup was inviting, as always. Soft, crunchy, slightly meaty, just a bit on the bland side but poised to wake up with the addition of a spot of red chile in oil. My palate has total recall of that one.

The lighting in the restaurant was typical—fluorescent and bright—what Bobby used to call, "like the inside of an icebox." And because it was so bright, my eye was drawn to Hank's earring. I had noticed it before, of course. But it really sparkled in the fluorescent glare.

"I like your earring," I said. "I always thought emeralds were nifty. And it looks really good with your eyes." Hank's eyes are a lovely blue/green shade that lights up when he laughs. Which, fortunately, he does often.

"Oh, thanks. I got it in a little shop in Provincetown. Steve and I were there the summer of '76."

"You got that from Doris? At One of a Kind?"

"Yes, that was the name of the shop. Do you know it?"

"Sure do. Bobby and I were there that summer, too. The *whole summer*, if you can believe it. Quite an experience. Was Steve tall and lean with a gentle face and soft brown hair? Looked like a dancer?"

"That's about right. Here, let me show you a picture of him." Hank produced a snapshot from his wallet. I wondered why I had never seen the picture before, in the year we had been "dating." My breakup had been so public, but Hank's loss was deeply private.

"Well, now I know why you've always looked familiar to me. Bobby and I were in Doris's shop when you bought that earring. We were looking for a baby gift, and guess who the baby was? None other than the big baby who's moving into my apartment after Christmas! I couldn't help noticing you as Doris pierced your ear. And then Steve was supposed to have *his* ear pierced, but he backed out!"

"He sure did."

"Now I can remember it as clearly as if it were yesterday. I thought you two must be very much in love."

"Yes, we were."

"And so were Bobby and I."

"Yes."

"And yet, if I had the courage, I'd have walked right up to you and planted a big kiss."

"How about tonight, instead?" Hank asked.

"Good timing," I answered.

After dinner, Hank and I went to his apartment and got right to that kiss. And then some more kisses. And we've been doing it ever since. How is it going, this new life? It's wonderful. What about the past? Also wonderful. For the most part. Would I dodge any of it, given a choice? Not a chance. Every minute with Bobby was precious. Even the terrible ones.

Have I healed? Sufficiently to find joy in every day. How about the heart? The scar tissue is thick, but the rest of it is stronger than ever. Any regrets? Of course, but none I can't handle. Guilt? A fact of life; a permanent condition. Love? Enduring.

The End

This is a first edition from
Audacity Books
Please visit us on the web at
www.audacitybooks.com
For information, please send your request to
info@audacitybooks.com.

This is Volume III of Bruce K Beck's **Love Trilogy.**
*AND LOVE ENDURES*, is set in the early 1990s.
*LOVE AND THE EPIDEMIC*, set in New York City in the
mid-'80s, is Volume II. And Volume I,
*YOU'RE SURE TO FALL IN LOVE*, is set in Provincetown,
MA, in the summer of 1976. For updates, please subscribe at
www.audacitybooks.com.

Many thanks to Sonya Teclai, Social Media Director at Audacity
Books, for her support throughout the project. Particular
thanks to Kathie DeNobriga, Lukas Hassel, and Walter Maas
for their generous wisdom. And to Richard Kutner for his
classy edits. Tim Barber of Dissect Designs (www.dis-
sectdesigns.com) signed on as a cover designer and became a
friend. You're sure to fall in love, indeed. This journey would
not have been possible without the example and the teaching of
Joanna Penn at www.thecreativepenn.com. I am delighted, Joanna, to add this volume to your long list of books you have
enabled. No doubt you will hit your one million mark any day
now!

Readers are invited to listen to the
YOU'RE SURE TO FALL IN LOVE Playlist at
www.youresuretofallinlove.com

Bruce K Beck is both a writer and an accomplished chef. His novels are available at amazon.com/author/brucekbeck and other places books are sold. Before turning to fiction, Beck authored **PRODUCE: A FRUIT AND VEGETABLE LOVERS' GUIDE**, which was called "gorgeous" by **The New York Times**, "a dazzler" by **Bon Appetit**, and "the most spectacular food book of the year" by **The Boston Globe**. His next book was **THE OFFICIAL FULTON FISH MARKET COOKBOOK**, which was called "invaluable" by Jacques Pépin, and "a treasure" by Irene Sax of **Newsday**. And Rex Reed said, ". . . you'll love this book. It's like a movie!"

📖

www.ingramcontent.com/pod-product-compliance
Lightning Source LLC
Chambersburg PA
CBHW021020120726
47905CB00009B/3098